SWAMPED!

JOE TENNIS

JCP

Jan-Carol Publishing, Inc

"every story needs a book"

For Daniel & Jim

Swamped!
Joe Tennis

Published October 2018
Little Creek Books
Imprint of Jan-Carol Publishing, Inc.
All rights reserved
Copyright © 2018 by Joe Tennis

ISBN: 978-1-945619-72-4
Library of Congress Control Number: 2018957366

You may contact the publisher:
Jan-Carol Publishing, Inc.
PO Box 701
Johnson City, TN 37605
publisher@jancarolpublishing.com
jancarolpublishing.com

SWAMPED!

ALSO BY JOE TENNIS

Haunted Highlands
Ghosts & Legends of North Carolina, Tennessee, and Virginia

Along Virginia's Route 58
True Tales from Beach to Bluegrass

Virginia Rail Trails
Crossing the Commonwealth

Washington County, Virginia
Then & Now

Finding Franklin
Mystery of the Lost State Capitol

Haunts of Virginia's Blue Ridge Highlands

Sullivan County, Tennessee
Images of America

The Marble
and Other Ghost Tales of Tennessee and Virginia

Southwest Virginia Crossroads
An Almanac of Place Names and Places to See

ACKNOWLEDGMENTS

The author gratefully acknowledges the assistance and suggestions of Linda Hoagland, Sylvia Nickels, Carol Jackson, Maggie Caudill, Janie C. Jessee, Tara Sizemore, David McGee, Dave Sadowski, Mike West, and Judith Rosenfeld.

CHAPTER 1

"This sucks. This really sucks. You *know* it sucks. And I'm not putting up with it anymore. I'm serious."

"Shut up," Tom said to me. "I ain't got time for your wimpy complaints."

Tall, curly-haired Chris moaned something from his seat at the stern of our boat. And it was something stupid, like, "Maybe we shoulda brought another oar."

Chris then turned to Justine, the young blonde on the boat seat beside him. "Like," he mumbled, "if Tommy doesn't get the boat fixed then maybe we could, like, have a little kiss."

Justine giggled. "Maybe later," she promised.

Tom howled, "It ain't the dang boat that's broke! It's the oar!"

"Oh, stop it!" I exclaimed. "You know, every time you push that oar it slings mud on my arm."

Standing up in the boat, Tom sighed and looked at me like I had a problem.

Disgusted, I turned the other way as the wind's wail increased. Our tiny boat drifted on the flat saltwater creek, inching further toward what looked like open waters. If we went too far, Tom said, we could be cast adrift on an open bay and possibly lost at sea.

"I think we're gonna hafta beach this vessel," Tom announced.

"Oh, you're a real maritime expert, aren't you?" I snapped.

"Look, stupid," Tom shot back. "There ain't no way we're gonna move this boat all da way back to the campground on only one oar."

"Oh, come on, Tommy," Chris interjected. "You shoulda thoughta that before you broke the other oar!"

"What? I didn't break the other oar!" Tom exploded.

"Yes, you did!" I said. "You did! You did!"

"What? Now, look; you were oaring," Tom said, pointing at me.

"*Oaring?*" I said incredulously.

"OK, you were *rowing*," Tom corrected himself, "the boat when the oar cracked, and then you handed the oar to me and said, 'Row the boat.'"

"Technicalities," I said. "Still, it's your fault, Tom. You broke the oar."

"Look, Apple Jelly—" Tom started saying but suddenly stopped when the boat began shaking.

I could only sigh. Then I thought about it. I guess Tom was right about one thing: We were not going to make it back to the camp with only one oar. No, not against that wind. We had gone about one mile, and now the wind was so strong that it seemed to be pulling our boat into that wide, open bay.

Looking around, all I could see were banks of marsh and cottonwood trees. This looked like a swamp.

"Quit shaking the boat!" Tom shouted at Chris and Justine.

The couple would not listen. Chris simply tickled his fingers over Justine's soft-looking jeans.

"Ah, son-of-a-" Tom suddenly hollered as his legs tripped each other. His whole body plunged, head first, into the murky, fast-moving water.

Chris laughed as Tom started to splash, getting us wet. By then, Tom was flapping his arms in the green-looking water, looking like he was trying to fan flames. He also gasped, coughed, and shook water all around his head.

"Chris!" Tom shouted, after finally finding his feet on the creek bottom. "Beach the boat, Chris. We can't make it back. There's no way."

"But, like, what if somebody drowned?"

"Then die then!" Tom screamed breathlessly, spitting his words with a whole lot of water.

Oh, what a jerk, I thought.

I turned away as Chris moaned, saying something about how he had to turn our sole surviving oar into a paddle. Drudgingly, Chris clumsily slammed our rowboat into the shore, at a place packed with mud and lined with reeds.

The side of the boat—portside, maybe starboard (I don't know)—drifted a bit and banged against the bank. Chris told me to grab the bow line, and I tied the rope to a cottonwood tree just within my reach. It scraped my arm, but I didn't stop to complain. I simply shivered, and oh, how I wanted to scream!

That cold, April wind felt like a breath of death. And the choppy waves licking the side of the boat pounded fear in my heart.

"What now?" Chris said.

Tom did not answer. He just went on this coughing kick, clearing his throat and spitting. Finally, a long minute later, he sloshed ashore, looking like a soaked-to-the-gills sea urchin returning from the deep.

Kicking some vines out of his way, Tom tromped over to our boat, which Chris struggled to hold still by clinging to a cottonwood branch, all the while holding Justine's left hand.

Standing over us and looking down at the boat, Tom started laughing with deep, hearty roars.

"What's so funny?" I asked.

"It looks like we're gonna walk," Tom announced.

"Walk on the water?" Chris said.

"You mean we really have to walk through all this nature

3

garbage?" I asked.

Tom sighed and rubbed a hand across his wet hair. "You guys are morons," he said.

"Oh, yeah, right," I replied. "Was it not your idea to go out in this boat?"

"And weren't you the one who broke the oar?" Chris added.

"Hey, look," Tom fumed. "All I said was 'Wanna go in the boat?' And these two lovebirds fell into the thing all gooey-eyed—"

"Gooey-eyed?" I interrupted.

"And you..." Tom pointed at me, shaking his head.

"Yeah, what?" I said.

"I already told ya," Tom said, "we gotta go hikin' until we make it back to camp."

"All of us?" I asked. "What, can't you go alone?"

"Yes, all of us. Because we're all in this together," Tom said. "Everybody said they wanted to go, so here we are."

"Like, in the middle of nowhere," Chris said with a moan.

Justine suggested we wait for help.

"No," Tom said. "Nobody knows we're here. And if we wait, it's only gonna mean we're waiting for a storm."

We all looked at the sky, eight eyes scanning its scary, purple hue. That horizon appeared to be only minutes from exploding with rain.

A few seconds passed before Chris got out of the boat. Next, Tom and Chris pulled the boat on the bank. But I did not help. I honestly did not want to get in the middle of what looked like quite a muddy task, so I just stayed idle with Justine until Tom told us to get out, too.

Getting up on land, I felt scared. I was also annoyed. This swamp felt sticky and sweaty. And all I could see were brown, dead, marsh stalks spanning endless fields.

But the bank near our feet, well, at least that did bear some signs of civilization. I noticed a Styrofoam cup, a messy clump of fishing-pole string, and what interested Tom: some old beer cans. Tom told us that he liked the cans because he was a beer can collector.

Me? I just looked around at the whole place and sighed.

I mean, here we were: four teenagers from the suburbs, three boys and one girl. None of us knew anything about what to do next. Not really. And all that our leader, Tom, wanted to do was play with beer cans.

"This sucks," I said. "This really sucks. You know it sucks. And I'm not putting up with it anymore. I'm serious."

"Ah, jus' hold on, Apple Jelly," Tom said to me, all the while preoccupied with picking up those nasty cans.

Apple Jelly was this stupid nickname Tom called me because it sounds kind of like my real name. I didn't mind being called a condiment for toast—except when we were in public.

"Uh," Chris said, "I don't think you're gonna find any beer in those cans, Tommy."

"No," Tom said, hiding a laugh. "I don't think I am."

I sighed and asked what was going on.

"We need to start walking," Tom announced.

"You're crazy," I whispered.

Nobody heard me.

Chris put his arm around Justine and said, "I think we oughta either get back in the boat or go through these woods and see if the Coast Guard is around."

"Coast Guard," Tom mumbled.

"I'm serious," I said.

Justine suggested we leave a note. "But," she asked, "what do we write with?"

Chris suggested slicing somebody's finger and writing with blood.

"Nobody's slicing my finger," I said.

"Mine neither," Justine agreed.

5

Tom ruffled a little, sighing like he was huffing and puffing. Then, looking a bit like an impatient mad dog, he ripped open a little, red toolbox he had on the back seat of the boat. "We'll figure a way out of this bottle," he said as he grabbed an ink pen, and scribbled some words on a white vinyl seat cushion:

> *HELP!*
> *Oar broke upstream*
> *—drifted—*
> *Went to find new oar. Will be back*
> *around 2:00. Please send help.*

The last couple of lines looked faint on the cushion. The blue ink of that pen actually gave me an ominous feeling: Our time, like that ink, was drying up.

CHAPTER 2

Treading atop matted straw and soggy marsh, we picked and pushed our way through prickly vines and curly brush. Briars reached up and caught our legs. Still, somehow, Tom seemed adept at leading us through this no man's land.

Throughout the first few minutes of the walk, Tom babbled a stream of stale stories about how he and a friend used to take walks through swampy areas just like this. But I hardly listened. Why? Because I just did not care what Tom said about sticker vines, beer cans, marsh bugs, or any of that junk. And I certainly did not care to hear how this swamp compared to somebody else's.

I just wanted to go home.

All along, while we walked, Chris and Justine traded off carrying a red-and-white plastic cooler. Every once in a while, one of them would yelp an occasional "Ouch!" from getting stuck on a briar. I yelped, too. But Tom never did. Oh, no.

Tom was tough.

"What am I gonna tell my ma?" Chris said.

"Tell her we got a busted oar," Tom replied.

"This is so typical at this campground," I muttered. "I never should have come here to begin with."

"Well, what made you?" Tom asked me.

"I just wanted to get away from my mom," Justine broke in

with a lively tone. "She doesn't even know I'm out here."

"She doesn't even know you're here?" I asked.

"Nope," Justine said with a giggle.

"Well, maybe she's busy," I said.

"Busy going from guy to guy," Justine said.

To that, I did not know what to say. I just did not know how to relate. I mean, I came from a good home: mom, dad, dog, brother. Justine's world appeared to be nothing like that.

Yet just as soon as Justine spilled her guts about whatever shipwreck of a life she had at home, our shipwrecked rowboat captain, Tom, simply stopped strutting.

Tom approached the marsh closest to the creek and then dropped to his knees beside some holes in the ground. "You know what these are?" he asked, pointing.

"Holes," I guessed in a bored tone. "Just a bunch a' dumb, stupid holes."

Tom hunkered down, furtively. "Do you see the crabs moving?" he whispered. "They're called fiddler crabs. And they live in these little mud holes."

Now lying on the muddy bank, Tom put his hand behind one hole and pulled up a crab.

"See this guy?" he said. "See that? He guards the female with his big claw. The girl crab has only two small claws. But he has a big claw and a little claw."

"Why is that?" Justine asked.

"Just a lesson of nature," Tom said with a smile. "The man is the protector."

"That crab is like a guard," Chris said. "He wants to guard the girl, just like I want to guard you, Justy."

"That seems sexist," Justine said with a giggle.

"How so?" Tom asked.

"Like, how can she defend herself?" Justine said. "She needs a big claw, too, doesn't she?"

Tom smiled as he let go of the fiddler crab. Then, like he was showing off, he reached down to grab another crab out of another hole.

"Gotcha!" he said. "See? This is the girl. She has two small claws."

"What is this, a science lesson?" I asked sarcastically.

"These are kind of like swamp ants," Tom said.

"Swamp ants?" Justine said, giggling.

"Why would they be *swamp* ants?" I said. "Aren't there, like, regular ants out here, too?"

"Yeah," Tom said, "but maybe today, we are all swamp ants."

"Why is that?" Justine asked with a smile.

"I am not an ant," I protested defiantly.

"Yes, you are," Tom said, talking to me. "We're all ants in this world. It's what Thoreau says: a microcosm. We're all in this together."

"Oh blow! You know Thoreau?" Justine said with a big guffaw. "I mean, *Walden*... I read that. So super cool."

"Thoreau?" I asked.

"Yeah," Tom said. "Henry David Thoreau, the great writer, the great philosopher. Remember him, in English class?"

"Yes," I said. "But that's school stuff. And we are not in school. Why would you talk about school stuff like that?"

"Like what?" Tom asked.

"School stuff, now," I said. "That is so stupid, to talk about stuff from school when we are not in school."

"All of life is a school," Tom said. "We're all learning from each other."

"Yeah, well, not me," I said. "I don't even want to think about it."

Tom stood up from the marsh, and Justine grabbed the crab from his hand.

"Oh, she's cool," Justine said. "I'm taking her with me, the little swamp ant."

"What?" Chris asked.

"I'm going to save her," Justine said. "She needs me. She can't defend herself."

Tom laughed a little as he finally got off the ground and started to lead the hike again. Justine followed in second place, cradling her crab with both hands. Chris walked behind Justine, rarely taking his eyes off her behind. And I followed at the end, sighing with frustration.

"Ow!" Justine said after about two minutes. "Don't pinch me!"

Justine kept walking but said "Ow!" again in less than 30 seconds.

That is when Justine stopped walking, and apparently dropped her fiddler crab.

"Ooh, ick!" I said, looking at the ground below my feet. "It's your stupid ant!"

"What?" Tom hollered.

"It's a crab," Justine said.

"Oh, it's crawling," I said. "Get it!"

"Get what?" Tom asked.

"Augh!" I said then smashed that crab with my foot.

"Did you just kill it?" Tom asked. "Why did you kill that crab?"

"It was under my foot," I said. "I walked on it."

"Dude, you smashed it!" Justine said.

"You killed an innocent crab," Tom said.

"Whatever!" I shouted. "What does it matter?"

"You're tearing up stuff," Justine said.

"It was, like, a spider," I told them.

"You called it an ant," Tom said.

"You called it an ant!" I shouted. "Then you said everybody was an ant!"

"Well, what did it ever do to you?" Justine asked me, her piercing blue eyes staring stonily in my face.

"It was a bug. It was crawling," I said loudly. "And it freaked me out."

"It was no bug," Justine said. "Dude, it was a pet."

"Then why did you drop it?" I shouted. "What were you doing with it?"

"I was going to keep it," Justine said. "I was trying to save its life. Then it pinched me."

"So you dropped it," I said.

"It pinched her," Chris said, looking at me. "That crab hurt Justy. Nobody hurts Justy."

I sighed in frustration and shouted, "You called it an ant!"

"It wasn't an ant," Tom said quietly.

"But you called it one!" I yelled, then just stood there without another word, panting.

I just wanted it all to stop.

Thankfully, it did—after a moment of silence.

Tom made a proclamation, "Death comes to the swamp," then said no more.

CHAPTER 3

I stared down as we walked. I didn't know where else to look.
"What if there are snakes?" Justine wondered aloud, after about
three minutes of silence.

"They're probably in the water," Chris said. "I wouldn't know
if they're in the marsh grass."

"No snakes," Tom promised. "It's too cold for 'em."

"My brother once got bit by a snake," Chris said. "He said it
got on his arm and wouldn't let go, and then he hadda go to da
hospital..."

No one replied.

"My mother kept asking 'Is he gonna live?' But nobody told
her," Chris said. "I wanted something to eat 'cause we saw my
brother, but his eyes were glassed over, and his tongue slobbered
spit on his shirt. My mother tried to touch his hand, but his skin
was real cold. And the doctor told her he was in a coda—"

"A coma," Tom said.

"Yeah, one of those," Chris said. "But he was, like, asleep or
dead or something. Somebody said the snake felt like nails in your
veins—"

"Shut up!" I shouted. "You're making me sick!"

"We're stuck even if we do see a snake," Tom interjected. "Ole
Snakeface Savalas back at the camp, he said you can't kill a snake

until it bites ya."

"Huh?"

"Yeah," Tom continued. "According to that guy, that camp guard, he says there's this five-hundred dollar fine for killing snakes."

"Well, I don't care about any stupid weirdo at that stupid camp," I said. "All I know is I better not get bit."

We fell silent again, and, in that silence, I simply stared down at my footsteps. The roots of the cottonwood trees growing along the creek looked like cottonmouth snakes, to me. But I wasn't sure. I mean, I knew what a cottonwood tree was, but I didn't really know what a cottonmouth snake was.

Still, every time I heard the electricity-like hum of the bugs, I hunched up and nearly stopped walking. I got so scared once when a cricket chirped that I let out a girlish shriek. That shriek made Tom stop and ask what had happened. "Nothing," I told him.

For the next hundred steps, however, I was plagued by Chris and Tom's teasing: Hissing sounds seemed to lurk in every inch of the waist-high trees.

Walking on and on, we headed for what Tom kept calling north. Soon, we came into view of a long, winding tributary creek, branching off the banks of the creek that we had followed to land: the same fast-moving creek we had paddled through in the boat.

Strangely, and unlike the relatively repetitious ground we had just covered, this shore was beautiful. Fifty or more birds—ducks and seagulls—drifted atop the water's surface. We stopped far from that shore, however, because a thick, wet area of green marsh blocked our path.

Justine pointed to the marsh and said, "You wanna go through that?"

"Do we have to swim through it?" I wondered.

Tom answered us with a sneeze. "You don't want to swim

through water this cold," he struggled to say.

"You're gonna get sick," Justine warned.

"I know," Tom said, "thanks to Chris wanting to turn the rowboat into Casanova's Canoe."

Justine giggled, and Chris grunted, like maybe he thought Tom had taken a cheap shot at him.

I simply sighed with impatience. At that point, I just did not care about Tom's cold, or how he caught it. I didn't even care about this beautiful shore. I mean, even beauty can be tiresome.

Tom stood on his toes and looked all around. "What's that over there?" he asked, sounding excited as he peered into the distance. "In those pine trees, is that a log cabin?"

"Who cares," I mumbled.

"Well, that's where we're headed," Tom announced, not listening to me.

"But, like, what if this is some farmer's land and he kills us with his shotgun for trespassing?" Chris worried.

Tom didn't listen to Chris. He just started walking what he called east without a care.

We didn't follow him.

"I think Tommy's brain is frozen up," Chris said with a heavy laugh.

"I'm serious," I said.

"But if he thinks he knows where to go," Justine said, "then maybe he does."

"Oh, yeah *right*," I said.

"Look," Chris said, "Tommy's gonna do nothin' but end us up at some Bigfoot-type guy's house and then we all get shot from the trespassing."

"I'm serious," I repeated.

"Look," Chris said, "the water isn't that deep out there, I wouldn't think. Maybe we should split up: half of us go one way, and the other goes to whatever Tommy says is a cabin in the trees."

"No," Justine said. "I don't think we should split up."

"Do you like Tommy?" Chris said.

"What?" Justine asked.

I sighed with impatience. Honestly, Chris and Justine's deliberations were getting on my nerves.

"I think we should follow Tom," Justine said.

"No," Chris said. "I want you to go with me, Justy. I think me and you oughta go alone and see what we could do in the water..."

Hearing that, I looked away, scanning the marsh grass. Eventually, my eyes found Tom, now many yards ahead of us. He had gotten so far ahead that he looked small in the distance.

"What's he doing?" Chris asked, turning to see Tom standing idle and staring at the ground.

Chris walked away with Justine under his arm. I followed the couple, and we discovered Tom in contemplation about a long road of flat marsh. That marsh road looked amazingly clear, compared to the brush we had just passed along the creek bank.

"Have you three finished plotting ways to kill the czar?" Tom asked, not turning around as we showed up at his back.

"Why are you stopping?" I asked him.

"I don't like the way this looks," Tom said.

Tom placed one of his wet feet on the green straw. It crackled and shifted. Tom stepped back and announced, "It's filled with rats."

"So?"

"So, we turn back," Tom said.

"To the water?" Chris asked.

"No," Tom said. "I told you, it's too cold to go wading through."

"Maybe me and Justy could," Chris mumbled.

"Yeah, Tom," I joked, "maybe Chris does need a cold shower."

"I thought you said there weren't any snakes," Justine probed.

"No," Tom returned, "I just said it was probably too cold."

"Isn't it too cold for rats?" Justine asked.

"I dunno. I doubt it. Y'all can go tromping through that stuff if you want. But don't come screaming to me if you get bit," Tom said. "I just figure we oughta turn around and start out the other way. Maybe we can find a way to that cabin."

"Huh? No way!" I protested. "All you want to do is go slosh around these woods all day, like this was one of your G.I. Joe expeditions. I'm sick of it, Tom."

Tom looked at me with a cold face. "Do you want to lead?" he said.

To that, I turned away.

"I want to go through the water," Chris said. "We are lost. And that is the only way we can go."

"Did I say we were lost?" Tom returned. "No, I did not say we were lost. What I said was we ain't got no other choice but to turn around."

"You don't know what you're doing," Chris said then pushed Tom's right shoulder.

"What!" Tom snapped. "You wanna fight?"

Chris gave Tom another push. This time, Tom just shrugged back.

"You're all talk," Chris said.

"Hey," Tom said. "You can just save your 'He's all talk' routine—"

With that, Tom suddenly surprised us all with a push at Chris's shoulders. A startled Chris fell to his rump on the green-and-brown straw, looking embarrassed—especially in front of Justine.

I started laughing.

"Why don't we vote?" Justine suggested. "Vote for a leader."

"Or we can draw stalks," Tom said.

"Draw stalks?" Justine asked.

"Straws," Chris said as he got back on his feet, acting like nothing had happened. "I like straws. You can use those for the ice cream."

"What ice cream?" I said.

"The ice cream you eat with a straw," Chris said, brushing himself off.

"Yeah," Tom said, talking slowly. "But this is a swamp. We don't have any ice cream, and we don't have any straws. We have stalks."

Tom bent over to snag some marsh stalks. Then he held them out, explaining how we were going to draw stalks from my hand and whoever got the shortest one would be the leader.

That turned out to be Justine.

"So I guess you're it," Tom said.

"Oh, blow," Justine returned with a smile. "But I don't want it, you know? It's super cool. You do it."

"Me?" Tom said.

"What about me?" Chris asked.

Justine didn't say a word.

"We could still vote on a leader," I suggested.

"Yeah, but Justine is only fifteen," Tom said. "She's too young to vote."

"Chris is seventeen, and he's the oldest," I said. "I guess he's also too young to vote—legally."

"Stop it!" Chris said sternly. "I'm the leader now. It's my turn. I'm gonna be the one who leads us back to the boat."

"Well, go ahead," Tom said. "It would be good to have someone else share the blame."

CHAPTER 4

U gh," I moaned. "This is definitely not a place for golf tour-naments."

No one heard me. At least, no one replied. I don't know why I said that, anyway. I guess it was just a way to break up the tension we had shared from the time Chris took the lead.

In this silence, I felt strange. I mean, by this point, I was actu-ally beginning to enjoy the walk, almost like it had a purpose or something.

My socks were wet, my hair was sweaty, and I felt gross. But I was also beginning to feel like maybe God had something in mind for me. Maybe I was here to learn more about my friends. Or, since these guys were not really my friends, maybe I was supposed to make them my friends.

"You know," I said, trying to break the silence again, "getting into all this is icky and everything, but maybe when we get back we can all be friends."

"I thought we already were friends," Tom said, walking in the rear of the line.

"Well," I said, "you know what I mean."

"I do?" Tom asked.

"Well, you're sort of my friend, Tom. But you other guys cer-tainly are not."

"Really?" Tom asked. "And why's that?"

"You know," I said.

"No, I don't!" Tom exploded. "You're saying that Chris and Justine aren't your friends like you're ostracizing them, Apple Jelly. Do you draw specific lines and say, 'These are my friends, and these are just people?'"

"No," I replied. "I didn't say that."

"Well, what did you say?" Tom asked.

I sighed with agitation. "OK!" I conceded. "They're my friends too, Tom. Are you satisfied?"

Tom smirked. "Why would you politely lying, to say that you've lowered yourself to accept us swamp-hike trash into your social circle, in any way satisfy me?"

"Oh, you've really got a problem," I hissed.

"Really?" Tom asked.

"Yes," I said. "You're mad because Chris is leading the hike instead of you."

"No, Apple Jelly, I'm just mad at your prejudice," Tom said. "To me, a friend is someone you spend time with, and sometimes, do things with. Like, you and me and Chris and Jim have been staying at this campground for two days now, right? Well, unless somebody has to pass a test of loyalty or talk to you on the phone every day or pay dues, then I think we'd all pretty much be friends by now."

"Well, at least Jim had sense enough to stay in the trailer and not go in the boat," I said.

"What?" Tom snapped.

"Well, he's my friend... And I guess you're my friend," I said. "OK, OK. Chris and Justine are my friends, too."

"Oh? Really?" Tom gushed. "Congratulations, guys! You're Apple Jelly's friend."

I looked at Tom with confusion.

"What is it with you, Apple Jelly?" Tom said, attacking me

19

again. "A chameleon, that's what you are. You just change to whatever fits your surroundings. You're a boomerang! Did you say that Chris and Justine are your friends because you thought I wanted you to?"

"No," I said, still confused. Honestly, at this point, I had no idea what Tom wanted me to say, one way or another.

"Apple Jelly," Tom began again, "if you must be a chameleon, would you at least change to the color you believe in and not the one that makes you fit in?"

CHAPTER 5

A patch of dense cottonwoods closed our path a few minutes after Tom had verbally attacked me. There, at the onset of that patch, Chris stopped walking abruptly, causing Justine to fall into Chris and me to fall into Justine. Tom, in the back, stopped ahead of time. But all he did was stand there, laughing at the rest of us. For a moment, Chris appeared completely motionless. He just could not seem to admit that his way was the wrong way: a dead end.

Chris turned to Justine. She sighed and gave him a hug of encouragement. In turn, Chris slid his arms across her shoulders and onto her tiny back. Chris pulled Justine close to him and looked into her blue eyes, saying, "A thousand times and by a thousand other men have said what I say unto you, but as the river flows into the water, my heart pounds more love into my loins."

Justine gushed with red-faced embarrassment. "Like, happy to hear it," she said, then leaned up to allow her small mouth to meet his.

I smiled as they kissed and hugged each other. I was going to turn away, but that wasn't easy since we were all still in such close proximity; even with that buffoon Chris at the helm, a love scene in the middle of the same old cottonwood country was, I'll admit, impossible to ignore.

Tom, on the other hand, just went on laughing. It seemed like that egomaniac had absolutely nothing on his mind but to find a way out of our dead end. I'll bet he did not even notice how much Chris and Justine made steamy fools out of themselves.

"This might work," Tom suddenly said, peeling back part of a tree.

Cutting his hand on a sticker vine, Tom didn't stop to complain. He didn't even say "ouch." Dogmatically, he just tromped through everything to become our leader again.

Chris, meanwhile, sheepishly fell back into place without another word—this time, at the end of the line. As he did, I got to thinking about leaders. It seems to me that some people never actually admit they have screwed up their leadership; they just fade back into the ranks of the followers, hoping, I guess, that everyone will forget where they once stood.

CHAPTER 6

"H ome sweet home!" Tom sang, I'm sure with pride, when we caught our first glimpse of the boat minutes later.

Tom let out a stupid, soulful cheer then ran, high-stepping over a few briar patches, to reach our beached vessel. Like a hungry wild man, he ripped open the lid of his red plastic toolbox—which he had left behind on the boat—and grabbed his pack of cigarettes.

"Oh, you're not really going to smoke those stupid things, are you?" I asked.

Tom ignored me. He just stuck a cigarette in his mouth and lit a match.

Moving the fire to his cigarette, however, proved impossible: I kept blowing out his matches! But on his third try, and with a run of about twelve steps, Tom won.

"Must be quite a victory for you, to kill yourself with nico-tine," I chastised Tom, after another of his silly cheers.

"No," Chris perked up to say, "that's not what my mother says kills you. She's heard of a guy who bleeds when he smokes."

"Ooh!" I squealed.

"You know, my mother smokes," Justine said. "She smokes about a pack a day."

"A pack a day is, like, nothing," Chris said. "My mother used to know a guy who smoked nine packs a day! No, nine packs a week. I mean, all I know is he smoked a lotta cigarettes."

"Oh, shut up," I ordered.

"Huh?" Chris said. "You don't like me very much, do you?"

"No, Chris," Tom broke in, almost snarling. "He doesn't."

I didn't say anything to Chris or Tom, because you know what? They were right. I did not like him at all. I thought Chris was boorish, loud, and dumb. That's the truth. I got so tired of his jokes, and even just how he talked. There were times, I'm telling you, when I just could not stand looking at him. His hair looked wiry and wicked: a sweaty, curly mess reminding me of Medusa. Sometimes, I could see the back of his head when we walked, and it was spooky. It was like a snake was going to suddenly creep out of that hair and turn the whole world upside down.

That's what the swamp looked like, too: spooky. We were several yards away from the boat when Tom had us head into the wilderness, away from the water—without giving us a break.

"Chris just tells all these stupid, stupid stories," I finally decided to say.

"So you're saying Chris is stupid?" Tom asked as we walked.

I looked at Chris. Just then, I noticed he was much taller than me.

"Uh, no," I replied. "Did I say that? Stop putting words in my mouth, Tom. Why don't you just shut up and smoke your stupid cigarette?"

"Oh, so now my cigarette is stupid?" Tom asked, this time with a laugh.

"Oh, just leave me alone," I begged.

Tom laughed again.

I sighed and griped, "Why don't you like fresh air? I swear, Tom. Why do you want to clog your air up with that thing?"

"Because this cigarette, Apple Jelly, is more than just a thing," Tom said. "Why, set it afire and this little animal comes alive."

Tom puffed and breathed on his so-called animal. "And when

24

you are alone," Tom said, "the cigarette cures that loneliness. The cigarette becomes your friend."

Justine giggled.

"The cigarette is your friend?" I asked, not buying a word of Tom's nonsense. "I thought you were the one who went into that rant saying that we were all your friends. But now you are alone, Tom, and your cigarette is your friend."

"What?" Tom said. "I never said I was alone, Apple Jelly. The cigarette can still be my friend, even if I'm with y'all. It's just that now I have four friends with me."

"Oh, blow," Justine said, laughing. "Y'all are gettin' goofy."

"I'm serious," I said.

"Aw, Justine," Tom said slyly. "Fifteen years old? Baby, you're just jealous because you ain't sixteen like me and get to smoke a cigarette. It's against the law for you."

Justine laughed some more.

"Oh, you think I'm kidding?" Tom continued. "I'm as sure as I'm standing here that you'd give your eyeteeth to walk into a drugstore and have the cashier sell you some cigarettes. But no, baby; you have to be sixteen. Can't do it without it."

Tom took another puff. "I can see it now," he said. "Why, just yesterday, when we met you, there was little Justine and her junior-high pal, praying they could catch just one little head rush."

True story, that actually was how we'd met Justine the day before. Some kid on a skateboard had bummed one of Tom's cigarettes. Then Chris started laying all these dumb lines on Justine as Jim and I rode bikes down the campground road.

"That age thing is a rule," Justine said. "Rules just get in the way."

"No, you do need rules," Tom said.

I listened, but didn't say anything. I really didn't know what to say. I knew rules were important, but I did not know why.

"Rules hold us down in an uncomfortable world," Justine said.

"Yeah," Tom said, "but that's like your little skateboard buddy and his anarchy symbol. Does he even know what anarchy means? 'No rules,' I heard him say. 'We need a society without rules.' What an idiot. Doesn't he realize that with anarchy, he'll lose everything, including cigarettes? I mean, who is really going to stand in a hot field and pick tobacco in a land without rules?"

"Somebody might," Justine said. "Anarchy would still be better than a government that lies, fights wars out of greed, and steals all our money to buy new plates for the White House."

"OK," Tom conceded. "I'd like to get rid of our photogenic government. I mean, if I were president, appearance and fashion would be way down the list."

"You couldn't be president," I said to Tom. "You don't know how to dress."

Tom shook his head.

"All I know," Justine said, "is that if we didn't have a government, everybody wouldn't all be running around complaining about how much we owe."

"No," Tom said. "Nobody would owe anybody. Nobody would know anything. And nobody would live anywhere, because we would probably all kill each other."

"That's so cynical," Justine said, then sneezed.

"Maybe," Tom said to Justine. "But I think you're being short-sided to think we can exist with any form of anarchy. Really. And I'm sorry for sounding so narrow-minded, but anarchy just hits me wrong. I mean, we're living in the most spoiled country on Earth. It might not really be equal for everybody, or fair, but America is free."

Tom's voice became increasingly dramatic. "Boys and girls," he said, "in America, we are free to trudge through swamps, break oars, argue, laugh, cry, and yes, oh, please, we have the right to smoke cigarettes until cancer gives us death."

Tom paused, perhaps to revel in the glory of his speech.

"No, wait a minute," Chris said. "Weren't you the one who was smoking a cigarette the time you, me, and Jimmy went camping and you broke the window on the trailer door?"

Tom shook his head with a smirk. He didn't stop walking, he didn't say a word, and he didn't turn around.

"You broke a window at this camp?" I asked Tom.

"Yeah, last summer," Tom mumbled. "Chris was inside this camper with a girl, and he had the door locked. I wanted in, so I started banging on the window. Then all of a sudden, it just shattered."

"Peeping Tom," I teased.

"Nah, man," Tom said. "I was only trying to get my hat."

"Oh, the price of a hat," I said with a mouthful of giggles.

"Exactly," Tom said. "It cost me three bucks at a hardware store to get a new window pane—one that I had to install myself."

"So," Justine asked Chris, "you had the door locked with a girl inside?"

"Yeah," Chris said, sounding a little nervous, "but her name was Kimmy and she—"

"Her name was the Twilight Tramp," Tom announced. "Chris was laying the lines on her pretty smooth."

"Oh, you were, were you?" Justine asked anxiously.

"Uh," Chris hesitated, "like maybe... We were... All I know is that she was a girl—"

"That you had locked inside your trailer, right?" Justine said testily. "What were you going to do with her, Chris?"

"I dunno."

"Well, I think I do," Justine said, suddenly sounding infuriated. "I think I know pretty well! I think you were going to have your way with her, like you try to do with every girl you meet at this camp. Like, it must be a yearly ritual for you to come down here and see what your tan skin and curly hair can cling to!"

Agitatedly, Justine ran her fingers through her sandy-blonde hair. "I've got to hand it to you, Chris," she said. "Most boys have a car that runs out of gas. But you have a boat that runs out of oars!"

Justine tore away from our trail and ran into some wind-blown marsh clumps.

Chris ran after her.

I stopped walking.

"Ah, now what the devil is going on?" Tom turned his head to holler, looking determined to go on hiking without any of us.

I looked at Tom and hoped to change his brazen mood by teasing. "Justine claims Chris broke the oar," I said. "Should you not set her straight and admit that you were the one who actually broke the oar?"

"Don't start that crap with me again," Tom said with an exasperated sigh. Then he turned around and spit.

Tom's spitting made me sick. So sick, in fact, that I ran from Tom to go eavesdrop on Chris and Justine.

"I don't even know where she is now," I heard Chris say.

"Oh, is that how much girls mean to you? You just forget all about them?" Justine asked, her face hidden by her hands.

"I dunno," Chris said, nearly crying himself. "Justy, honey, I've known you for what? Two days, including today? And I like you like I like a bottle of pop; you're yummy good."

Justine uncovered her face and swallowed a tear. "Oh, Chris, really?" she asked.

"Uh-huh," Chris said from his goofy squatting position in front of her. "And when I want to be with you, I won't lock the door, OK?"

"Oh, Chris, shut up!" Justine exclaimed, and threw her left shoe at him.

"What? What's wrong?" Chris asked.

"You!" Justine said, her agitation evident in her voice. "You just assume that we're going to be together."

28

"But you said 'Maybe later' when I asked you before..."

Justine did not reply.

I looked up at the dark clouds, thinking about rain and our safety. Then I got an idea: Maybe we should leave these two morons behind.

I ran back to our leader. I found him smoking another cigarette.

"What are they talking about?" Tom said.

"*It*," I said, giggling.

Tom nodded like a befuddled father.

"Chris said he liked her as much as a soft drink," I said, "and then she hit him."

Tom let out a laugh, which blew cigarette smoke in my face.

"You know, this is your fault," I said.

"Hmm? Why's that?"

"Because you are the captain of our boat. And because you were the one stupid enough to say Chris wanted to fool around with whomever," I said and sighed. "You really need to learn some tact."

"Tact? What good would using tact do with hiding things?" Tom asked.

"Well, for one, an ounce of tact would show you have some sense and you know how to act a little bit civilized."

"Sorry, Mom."

I sighed and said, "You know what your problem is, Tom? You don't have a girl out here, like Chris does."

"Uh-huh..."

"And since you don't, you just want to go around upsetting everybody."

"And that's what wrong with me?" Tom asked.

I nodded.

"Apple Jelly," Tom said, "have you ever stopped to consider how young Justine is? I mean, all I told her was about how Chris got involved with that chick and how he can be. Isn't it better for her to know how he might be? Really, I don't see how me putting things bluntly is going to hurt. And really, I can't see why it would bother you so much."

"Tom, what bothers me is you'll say anything, to anybody, at any time."

"So?" he said. "It bothers me to see you mumble something behind somebody's back and then not have the guts to say the same thing to their face."

"Well, some things just don't bother me for long," I said. "And then I forget about them. I simply do not need to stir up trouble with somebody when I'll probably forget about it soon anyway."

Tom puffed on his cigarette. Although I was mad at him, I still found it funny to see how Tom smoked; he sprayed breath freshener on the filter to pretend he was smoking menthols.

"Well, I guess I won that argument," I decided to say.

"You won?" Tom asked in a testy voice. He seemed like a sore loser. "Just wait a second here. You and me, Apple Jelly, we're standing in the middle of a swamp, under a rain cloud, arguing about tact?"

With a smile, I answered, "It sure looks that way."

Tom nodded and crushed his cigarette in the dirt, and I checked to see that the fire was gone. Tom then stretched up his neck in a way that appeared that he was lightheartedly accepting the swamp's strangeness of things.

"But Tom..." I began.

"Hmm?" he said distractedly, drifting into thought.

"What do we do about those two?" I asked, pointing at Chris and Justine.

The couple was by then playfully dancing around the marshy field, throwing Justine's fallen shoe at each other.

Tom instantly slipped out of his soul-searching euphoria and fell into a disgusted cussing mode: swearing at Chris, swearing at the swamp, swearing at Justine's shoe.

"Don't get too close to her!" I heard Chris say. "She's a regular shoe-throwin' mama!"

What a jerk, I thought. I mean, it might have been funny to see this scene: Tom as the captain, Chris as the over-grown playboy and Justine as the new girl in town. But that stupid remark just made Chris look like a jerk.

CHAPTER 7

We were not friends—not me and Chris. I mean, I didn't even know Chris until three days before all this. I knew Tom from school for a couple of years. But really, we all just got lumped into this camping trip by Jim. He was everybody's friend, and it was his parents' time-share membership at this campground that allowed us to go camping. But for some reason, Jim didn't feel like going in the stupid boat. So Tom signed the checkout sheet, saying he would be responsible for getting the boat back. That made him the captain, I suppose. Chris asked Justine to go in the boat, and she said yes, figuring we were heading out for an hour. That's the same thing I thought when I went, too.

"Are we in the middle of nowhere?" I asked, just after we all started walking again.

"Yeah!" Justine said enthusiastically. "But who cares?!"

"I care," Chris said.

Justine giggled, then she sneezed again.

"I care about you," Chris said. "I always have."

"Really?" she asked.

"Uh-huh," Chris replied.

"Why?" Justine said.

"Why, why, why," Tom muttered.

"Why do you care?" Justine said as we leisurely walked through the mostly-dry wetlands.

"Because you are pretty," Chris said. "And because I have known you for a long time."

"Two days," Tom muttered.

"Two days," Chris said. "I have known you for the two best days of my life."

Ah, two days, I thought. It must have been love on two bikes, I figured, as I remembered how Chris, Tom, Jim, and I had rented these bikes at the camp and then raced up and down the paved roads, dodging old people and kids in the curves. Around lunch-time, we pedaled up to this lonesome-looking trailer near Hudson Lane, where Justine was staying with her mom and her grand-mother, who had a trailer to herself. Tom called Justine's grand-mother "the little old lady next door." She coughed a lot, and she covered herself with an afghan that had angels on it. That old woman looked scary.

"My mom is never around," Justine said, about a minute after we met her.

"Who is this?" Chris said, pointing to Justine's grandmother.

"Oh, her," Justine said. "She's around too much."

"What does she do?" Chris asked.

"She cramps my style," Justine said with a sneeze.

"'Cramps my style?'" I remembered mumbling that day, back at the camp. "'Cramps my style?' Who talks like that?"

But I still got it; I knew the intent. Justine was like us. We were there to be freewheeling teens and have fun. But Justine's grandmother gave us an evil eye, howling, "Don't race like that," as we tried to leave tire marks on the concrete driveway outside Justine's trailer.

"Where is your mom?" Tom had asked Justine, back at the camp.

"My mom," Justine said with half a laugh. "She's the butter-fly, going from guy to guy."

"I think that's terrible, your mom being gone," I said that day.

"I know my mom is always there for me."

Out in the swamp, I thought again about what I had said at the camp. It was a day later, and yes, I know what I said sounded a little preachy, but I still didn't see anything wrong with what I'd said. So, out in the swamp, I said the same thing again—to Justine.

"My mom?" Justine said, sounding startled that I had changed the subject. "Yeah, I think she knows what people say about her."

"I don't know how she could do that," I said. "I just could not take it. I couldn't take being called something by somebody else. I just want to be liked by everybody."

"It ain't gonna happen," Tom said. "Somebody always hates you, even if they're just jealous."

"Well, my parents are normal," I said. "Your parents are normal, too, aren't they, Tom?"

Tom didn't say a word.

"She cares about me, I think," Justine said. "My mom just gets all caught up with herself and her dudes. Like, who's in the next trailer, you know?"

"No," I said. "I don't know."

"She's searching," Tom said.

Justine smiled.

"Searching for what?" I said.

"Searching for herself," Tom said. "Or she's searching for a soul mate."

"Oh, blow," Justine scoffed. "I know everybody wants that. But is that really what you get?"

"Sure," Tom said. "Soul mates are real. I mean, without a soul mate, where would songwriters be? Where would poets be? Nobody would have ever written a great song or poem without the dream of finding a soul mate. It's like the great dream of Eden."

"I could be your mate," Chris mumbled, the first words he'd spoken in several minutes.

"You're definitely the first mate," Tom said.

"Not for you, Tommy," Chris said. "I'll be Justy's mate."

"I mean," Tom said, "you're the first mate on our boat."

"Some boat," I said. "You wrecked it."

"Swamped it," Justine said, laughing.

"Yeah," I agreed. "Swamped! That's what we are. We are swamped."

"Swamped?" Tom said. "That means to take on water."

"Well, we're taking on water," I said.

"More like stuck," Justine said. "Stuck in a swamp."

"Stupid swamp," I said.

"I'm serious," Tom said, then pointed to me and laughed.

"So, we're shipwrecked?" Chris said.

"No, we're swamped," I said, laughing.

"Well, not for long," Tom said. "I think we're just about on the brink of our rescue."

"Really?" I said, smiling. "How is that?"

"Up ahead," Tom said, then ran a little bit beyond all of us. "I see something."

"What?" Chris said. "The camp?"

"No," Tom said. "How the—no, there's no way. The camp is on the other side of the creek, remember? We would have had to swim across the creek to get back."

"So?" I said.

"There's something up ahead," Tom said. "I think it's that cabin."

"Well, it better be," I said. "Or, else, we are just running around out here all day on one of your wild goose chases."

"I ain't chasing geese," Tom said to me. "There are geese out here, but I ain't chasing them."

"You are a birdbrain, though," I said, joking a little. "All you ever want to talk about is birds."

"Like seagulls?" Justine said. "Man, I love seagulls."

"Do you love me?" Chris said.

"Oh, come on," I mumbled.

"Do you?" Chris said.

Tom stopped and put his arm around Chris. He said, "I love ya, pal."

"I'm talking about Justy," Chris said, pulling away from Tom.

"I'm not in love with Justy," Tom said.

Justine giggled. "Love's crazy!" she said, smiling as bright as the sunshine. "It's just crazy!"

"Crazy?" Tom said, smiling at Justine.

"Super crazy," Justine said. "That's what love is."

Tom stopped and simply smiled at Justine.

"Stop it, Tommy," Chris said.

"Stop what?" Tom asked innocently.

"You like my woman," Chris said.

"Woman?" I said, laughing a little.

"Yeah, wow. I ain't exactly a woman," Justine said, giggling. "Oh, blow. That's like, a *major* not-yet, man."

"She's my girl," Chris said.

"I thought you said she was a woman," Tom said.

I laughed, and so did Justine.

But Chris did not. Not at all.

Chris exhaled, and he sounded like a dragon clearing his throat. Then he reached down and picked up a stick.

"This is my sword," Chris said. "I will fight you."

"Fight me?" Tom said, still laughing. "Fight about what?"

"Justy," Chris said. "She is mine."

"With a stick?" I said, laughing a little.

Tom turned to look at Justine, like he wanted her to say something.

"What?" asked Justine.

"What?" Chris asked.

"What?" Tom said.

"That's what I what to know," Chris returned. "I want to

know what you have in mind."

"With what?" Tom said.

"I just think he's trying to lead us," Justine suddenly said, breaking the impasse by speaking directly to Chris. "We're all friends here."

"Yeah, well, not according to Apple Jelly," Tom said.

"What?" I asked. "What did I do?"

"Friendship," Tom said flatly, looking at me with a sour expression.

Chris dropped his stick.

"Forget it," he said. "We'll just call this a duel."

"A duel or a draw?" asked Tom. "Is this a draw?"

"Look, Tommy, I ain't drawing nothing, you hear me?" Chris yelled. "No line in the sand, Tommy. No line in the sand. You just lay off Justy."

Tom smiled and said, "You got it, pal. You got it."

CHAPTER 8

Silence came between us again, lasting another five minutes. We hiked through toe-deep water and more marsh, then stopped at the edge of a mini-forest of pines.

"Is this it?" I asked. "Where is it?"

Tom sighed. I could tell from the sound of that sigh that he really did not want to answer my question.

"Is this it?" Chris broke in. "Are we home yet? What is this? Is this that house? I don't see no house."

"Is this your cabin?" I said.

"I don't see no house," Chris said again. "All I see is trees."

Tom ignored us. Jogging ahead, he sat down on a log.

"I don't see no house," Chris said a third time.

"No," Tom said quietly.

"So now what?" Chris said. "I told you we shoulda gone another way."

"Oh, yeah," I said. "That's right; you wanted to go swimming."

"Geez," Tom mumbled. "I could have sworn there was gonna be something here."

"Maybe you saw a ghost," Chris said.

"A ghost cabin?" I said, laughing. "Like a whole house showed up?"

"Super crazy," Justine said as we three walked over to the log where Tom sat.

"So now whatta we do?" asked Chris.

Tom hunched his shoulders like all hope was lost.

Chris asked if anyone had a compass.

No one replied.

Chris held out his right palm and said, "I've always heard that when you get lost, all you need is a compass. You just point to it. And it's supposed to tell you where to go."

Tom shook his head with a grin and said, "Sorry, pal."

"So how do we know where to go?" Chris begged. "Do we have a map?"

"A map?" Tom perked up with a laugh. "Chris, I don't think anyone's ever even been in this marsh before."

"Oh," Chris said. "So now whatta we do?"

Tom sighed and shook his head again.

Nobody said anything for a solid minute.

"Uh-oh," I said, breaking the silence.

"What?" Tom said.

"I think I have to..."

"One or two?" Tom asked.

"One," I said.

"So? What's the problem?" Tom said. "If it was number two, you'd have to use leaves for toilet paper."

"Oh," I said quietly.

Thirty silent seconds passed.

"Are you just gonna stand there?" Tom said.

"Huh?" I panicked.

"Just do it!" Tom ordered.

"I can't," I said. "It is too embarrassing."

"Why? Because of Justine?" Tom said.

"No, it's everybody," I said, quietly.

Tom sighed again, this time sounding mad. "Apple Jelly!" he shouted. "Just go pee in the woods!"

"I can't," I said. "It's disgusting."

"Then shut up," Tom said, letting his back fall across that log.

I stopped talking. And, in the pines, I decided to rest. I faintly noticed Chris and Justine staring into each other's eyes as I lay back on the pine straw, gazing at the trees above my head. "I could sleep now," I mumbled, "but I know we have to keep walking."

"I would sleep with you," Chris said, apparently talking to Justine.

"What do you mean?" she asked.

"I could sleep next to you and hear your heartbeat," Chris said, reaching to touch Justine's left hand.

"And that's all?" she said.

"That's all I want," Chris said. "All I want is your heart."

No one said a word as another silent minute passed.

"Just go on," Tom said carelessly.

Chris and Justine disengaged from their embrace.

We all looked at Tom.

"Just leave me here!" Tom cried with a look of despair in his eyes. "I was the one who got us stuck..."

Tom sighed. He looked possessed. "Forget it," he said sternly. "I make myself sick, carrying on like an un-couth punk. And like it's really gonna matter if I rush back to the mall."

None of us could take our eyes off Tom.

"Stop it!" Tom shouted. "Quit staring at me! Gettin' us lost in this whatever-this-is. Carrying on all this teenage crap about government and liberty and anarchy—"

"Stop it!" Justine shouted at Tom.

Tom looked at Justine, his eyes swollen with tears. Then he turned and stared at the pine tree tops in the sky.

"Why?" he asked. "Why can't I get things right?"

"Well, you want to get us out of this swamp," Justine said, not taking her eyes off Tom's face.

"No," Tom said with a sharp pout. "No, I don't. We are swamped."

More tears flooded Tom's face until he opened his eyes wide like he was forcing them. "Lord!" he howled, apparently in prayer. "Please, help us!"

CHAPTER 9

No one said a word after Tom's prayer—not even Chris, who I swore was going to moan a stupid football cheer, shouting "AAAAAY-MEN!" and sounding like he wanted to bring attention to himself rather than God.

I shouldn't judge another about his faith, but those overly-enthusiastic, show-off amens just sound blasphemous to me. It's like, "AAAAAY-MEN! And pass the cookies!" It really bothers me, I think, because I feel sorry for people who think a loud, obnoxious "Amen!" is all they need to say—or that it will make up for them not listening to the prayer in the first place.

It took about three minutes for the rest of us to comfort Tom and get him on his feet again. Truthfully, though, Justine did all the work. She gave Tom a couple of hugs and tried standing him up. At first, he seemed clumsy and tripped on the pine straw. But Tom did eventually find his feet, and, as we should have guessed, he immediately sprayed breath freshener on another cigarette.

Sitting on top of another log, Tom puffed away as he peered across the swamp like a forest ranger, telling us about a creek and some more pine trees. He also claimed his sense of direction had been given stronger inspiration, too, like his prayer had been answered.

Then he jumped down, and, thank God, he led us again.

Back on our way, the ensuing walk through the pines seemed pleasant as we passed over blankets of thick, sodden pine straw. Yet that wet ground, my soaked feet, and the darkness in the trees gave no inspiration to help with my problem. The wetness just made me think of water, which only intensified my need for a bathroom. I didn't mention this to the others, though; I was too afraid Tom would yell at me again, or that Chris would mumble something stupid.

Honestly, I didn't want them to think I was just another un-cultured animal like Tom. That guy had already walked away and urinated against some brush—twice. Justine probably saw what Tom did at least once. I actually didn't see it, but the whole idea just made me sick.

Yes, the swampy marsh was uninhabited and probably would be forever. But really, just think about raw human waste seeping into the ground. I mean, I think I would have died had I lived a hundred years ago, or whenever it was when they didn't have sewers and everything was dumped out the window, often right into the street. But Tom? Oh, I bet he would have loved it back then, and thought anybody who could not handle it had a weak stomach. Then again, he probably wouldn't have known any better. But at least I would have thought it was sick! And embarrassing, too. It's like you'd go outside and bury it, and everybody would know you had diarrhea if you buried a whole lot of it in one day.

We continued walking, and, soon, the pines were gone. We passed into another field of marsh grass, briar patches, and cottonwood trees. Fortunately, the ground was pleasantly dry, but the hike became déjà-vu boring. It was like we crossed the same ground over and over. There was no change from one step to the next. I sighed and kind of wished we could have stayed in the peace of the pines.

"Does anybody know what time it is?" Chris wondered.

"Probably about three-thirty," Tom answered.

43

"Oh," Chris said and fell nearly silent again. And I say nearly because, truthfully, Chris never shut up. He didn't speak clearly; he just kept mumbling, on and on. To Justine, he babbled some story about a fire hydrant in his old neighborhood, and told her how everybody on his block painted their initials on it. But one day, the city came along and pulled the fire hydrant out, prompting everyone to sign a petition to get it back. Chris said—or mumbled, rather—that he'd cried for days because something he "played with" had been taken away. He said the fire hydrant "left" when he was not looking. Justine asked what happened to the petition, and Chris said, "I don't really know, but my mother said it seems like you never get answers when something you love gets taken away."

Just in sight of another group of pine trees, Tom abruptly stopped walking. Then he fell forward on his hands and knees. He started gagging, coughing, and spitting, just hacking up a great big storm. It grossed me out so much that I turned away.

Then he puked.

"You gonna be all right?" Justine asked, then sneezed yet again. "Is it allergies? I've got allergies."

In reply, Tom puked once more.

Turning away, Justine hunched against Chris's brown leather jacket and pushed her face between his left shoulder and chest. I was so weary and sickened by Tom's illness that I, in turn, pushed my face against Chris's right shoulder. Chris did not say anything when I did. He simply told us, "I think Tommy's going overboard is making him get new-moan-yuck."

Justine and I kept our faces turned away from Tom. Really, we had to. If Tom wasn't puking, he was spitting, and no one dared go near him, for fear they would be soaked in saliva.

I did once turn Tom's way, and I caught the sight of a tear in Tom's eye. Perhaps it hurt Tom that he was the one who fell overboard and was soaked, cold, and feeling sick. And that we were not helping him.

I wanted to tell Tom, "If you're that sick, go home," but it would not have made any sense.

Then again, I thought his spitting was getting out of hand, like Tom was deliberately calling attention to himself and wouldn't stop until we clapped.

This puke-and-spit thing went on for about four minutes. And I knew someone had to break, but it would not be me. No way, I thought, *spit all you want, but I am not coming over and getting soaked*. And the way Tom was coughing and almost gargling in the back of his throat made the idea of mucus pouring down my jacket completely unappetizing, thank you very much. Being a comforting saint was not going to do me any good. It was not my problem. And stepping in the middle with a hand to hold would only give me the problem of a messy jacket.

Surprisingly, Chris soon disengaged himself from being our head-rest. He moved over to touch Tom's shoulders. Immediately, as I should have guessed, Tom's dramatic spitting performance ceased.

"Do you need me to get you some help?" Chris offered.

Tom turned around and looked at Chris with grateful eyes. "I'm just feeling cold," Tom said quietly.

Chris looked at the ground then at Tom again. "Here," Chris said, taking off his jacket. "You can put this on, and maybe you'll feel warmer."

Tom smiled, said "Thanks," and accepted the jacket.

Chris returned to Justine. At that point, he stood out from every-thing in his tight, white turtleneck. For a few seconds, I thought of Chris as some kind of saint.

Then I remembered it was Chris's fault that Tom fell out of the boat in the first place. Tom should not have been standing up, but it was Chris who shook the boat. Fact is, Chris owed Tom that jacket.

CHAPTER 10

I was the first to set foot in the second set of pines, though Tom soon stole ahead and regained his lead position. Actually, he ran toward a particular tree.

"Wait up," I called out.

Tom didn't slow down. He just bolted, like he wanted to show he still had plenty of life.

It wore me out to watch him. My tired feet felt no comfort in my soaked shoes. I was just about exhausted.

Tom seemed so happy when he climbed his newfound pine tree that I could have sworn he would kiss it. Instead, he pulled himself up into its limbs, about seven feet above the ground.

"Our fort! Our flags!" Tom shouted, his eyes focused on something in the distance. "Our home fire is still burning!"

"You mean you can see the camp?" I asked.

Tom cheered and climbed down, giving us a non-stop, rambling explanation about a tributary creek, trees, and something else. I was too elated with relief to want to hear all the nitty-gritty.

"So, we know where we are?" Chris asked.

"Well, no," Tom said. "Let's just say we know how to get where we're going."

"Well, hey; that's sure news to take to the bank," Chris said, then went back to mumbling dumb nothings in Justine's ear.

Chris seemed pathetic—inept, actually. His lanky legs could not manage to walk without hitting that cooler he carried, which I saw him open a couple of times. He also never stopped trying to talk Justine into kissing him again. "You said you loved me... I have all these feelings," he would say. "A man has needs."

Yuck! It all sounded so fake that I wanted to have the kind of puking party that Tom just had. But I blocked it out, and, for a moment, I lost myself in the fragrance of walking through this second set of pines.

These trees proved to be more enjoyable traveling ground than the marsh. But I cannot say the second set of pines surpassed the serenity of the first. Walking through the first group of pines was a new experience. Walking through these other trees was more like seeing the repeat of a movie; it is just not as fresh and alive the second time around. But at least the towering shade took away my fear of the clouds.

CHAPTER 11

"Wait a minute. Just stop. I got to do it," Chris abruptly announced to all of us. "All this walking. Makes me need it."

Tom stopped the hike. "What?" he bellowed, his voice almost echoing in the pines.

I turned to see Chris, hugging Justine by his side. Smiling, Justine looked sleepy all of a sudden, but also kind of like she was ready to have Chris's baby or something.

"Me and Justy want to sit down over there on the straw, and you know...relax," Chris said and let out a giggle that, I swear, made him sound like the dumbest person I had ever met.

"Relax?" Tom said, sounding bothered by the idea.

"Well, *sort of* relax," Chris said, with a deep-voiced guffaw.

"You fool!" Tom snapped. "Don't you know it's going to rain any minute?"

"I'm serious," I said.

"Well, we hadda wait for you when you was sick," Chris said.

"And you think that's the same?" Tom asked.

"I'm serious," I said.

"Look," Chris said, like he was bargaining. "I...like, you already said we know our way back to the camp. And we can get there, so I think we have time."

No one replied.

Again, Chris tried to convince Tom. "I *got* to do it. All this walking. Makes me need it."

Tom sighed, said "Scratch it!" and grabbed the cooler from Chris's hand. Almost like a guide, Tom pointed the couple to a dry-looking area behind a large log, then kicked some of the pine straw out of either envy or agitation. Next, Tom motioned me to join him at a place several yards away, and we sat down at the edge of the marsh.

As Tom sprayed breath freshener on another stupid cigarette, I asked him, "Why did you let them—"

"Me?" Tom broke in. "What'd I do? I don't know what they're doing over there. For all I know, they could be playing in the dirt."

"Oh, yeah; *right*," I said sarcastically, then pouted because Tom would not take me seriously.

Tom puffed on his cigarette. "Did you ever get up the guts to spring a leak?" he asked me.

My face revealed the truth with a smile. "No," I replied. "I thought I would wait."

Tom nodded, like this time he might do something decent and accept my decision.

Feeling edgy, I ached to turn around and see what Chris and Justine were doing. But, like Tom, I stared the other way, looking over the marsh.

Still, mulling over the scene, I mumbled, "If something *does* happen, it will be your fault, Tom. You are the captain. You might end up even having to marry her. I mean, you were the one who said they could go over there."

"What is it with you, Apple Jelly? Are you going to blame me when it starts to rain?"

"No," I said quietly.

"Just because I'm leading the hike, everything has to go on my back?" Tom said. "With something like this, you could have said something. Leader or not, you're part to blame. So don't blame me, blame yourself. Or just blame them."

I shriveled up, sorry I had ever said a word.

"Well?" Tom demanded.

"Oh, come on, please," I begged. "I don't want to argue. Why don't we look in the cooler and see if we have something to eat?"

"Oh, great!" Tom said, exhaling a dramatically wild-looking plume of cigarette smoke. "Just like a woman, ain'tcha? Always think you can solve a problem with food?"

"I am not a woman," I said.

"Man, you can't even spring a leak."

"No. I am not going to be laughed at," I said, standing my ground. "And I am not going to descend to your level of animalistic behavior."

"Are you still afraid of ten seconds of embarrassment?"

"Oh, what a winner *you* are." I delivered this statement with biting sarcasm. "The whole world is just a free-for-all, isn't it? You just let your so-called friends act like wild beasts. I mean, why don't you just go live in a hippie commune, with your outdated ideas?"

"Look," Tom said. "If you object so much to them, then why didn't you say something?"

"I did."

"What? That 'I'm serious' garbage? You just say that to fit in."

"Sometimes," I said.

"Well, if that's all you can say, if all you can do is echo the rest of the world, then you ain't fitting in, as far as I'm concerned. To me, I wouldn't even count you as being there."

"Well, what about you?" I said. "You really stopped them."

"They don't bother me," Tom said, sounding nasty, like I was the one who had the problem.

"They don't bother you because you don't have any morals," I said.

Tom shook his head.

"You are the captain," I said. "And, like I told you, it's your responsibility."

"What?" Tom said.

"If there is a result of, you know, then it might as well be yours."

"My what?" Tom said.

"You were the one who said they could go over there," I said slowly.

"To do what?" Tom said.

"What do you think they're doing?" I asked Tom.

"What do *you* think they're doing?" Tom asked me.

"Do you think they're doing what I think they're doing?" I asked.

"I don't know," Tom said. "I'm not you."

"But what if there's a baby?" I said.

"From what?" Tom asked me.

"From...you know," I said slowly.

"No," Tom said.

"From *that*," I said dramatically.

Tom smirked but did not immediately reply. At that moment, we both heard a bird squawk somewhere over the marsh.

"Uh-oh," Tom said.

"Uh-oh, what?" I snapped back.

"Sounds like a stork," Tom said.

"A stork? What is that?" I exploded. "Is that what you are call-ing me now, stupid and a dork? Is that what that is? So now I am a stupid dork? Or stork for short?"

"Stork for short," Tom said, repeating my words. "Stork for short!"

"So that is what I am?" I said.

"A stork is a bird," Tom said.

"Oh, so now I am a bird?" I said.

"I didn't say that," Tom told me.

"Well, what did you say?" I asked.

"I never said you were a stork," Tom said, talking slowly with gritted teeth. "I said there is a stork. It is a bird."

"That was a sea gull," I told Tom.

"No, it was probably an osprey or an egret," Tom said. "Those are actually the kinds of birds that are in marsh like this."

"What are you, like, a birder now?"

"A birder?"

"Yeah, a birder," I said. "Somebody who has nothing better to do than watch birds."

"I do like birds," Tom said then paused with half a grin. "I don't know that I watch them a lot."

"You are watching your stork thing like you love it."

"No," Tom said, still talking slowly. "I said that could have been a stork. You were talking about where babies come from."

"No," I said sharply. "I was not. And I would not."

"But that's why I mentioned the stork," Tom told me.

"No," I said. "That is when you called me a stork."

Tom sighed.

With all this bird business, Tom sounded almost silly, maybe even funny, but not then. Not with that sigh. That sigh sounded mean, like Tom was mad.

"I didn't do anything," I said, trying to break the silence.

"I know," Tom said flatly. "You never do anything."

I sighed, and I wanted to be mean—just like Tom.

"A stork," Tom said, sounding calm but a little testy. "A stork is a bird that delivers babies."

"Oh, yeah...right," I said.

"It's a legend," Tom said, attempting to smile. "It's an old, funny story that this big, white bird delivers babies. And that's where babies come from."

"Nuh-uh," I said. "You are just shifting the blame to some bird. How dumb, Tom. You know there is going to be a baby—a swamp baby—and it might as well be yours."

"What?" Tom said.

"You are the leader," I said. "Chris isn't any leader. He was talking about Bigfoot all day. And now he's over there."

"With a bird," Tom said. "Don't forget that."

"Huh?" I said.

"The stork," Tom said with a smile. "The one that's bringing the baby, remember?"

"Tom, you're dumb."

"I'm trying to be funny," Tom said with a smile.

"Well, you aren't," I said with a scowl. "You are not funny at all. You're just a bad leader. You should be more like a general."

"A general?"

"Like in the military," I said. "You should be more disciplined. But you aren't; you don't have any order. You just get us out here on this boat and crack that oar, and now we're swamped."

"And this is all my fault?" Tom said, no longer smiling.

"Well, I didn't do anything."

"I know," he said. "You never do anything."

"Well, I didn't crack the oar. You did."

"No, you didn't want to use the oar," Tom snarled.

"I did not even want to go out in the stupid boat!" I shouted.

"Well, why did you?" Tom asked me.

"I don't know," I said.

"Well, I don't know, either," Tom said.

I was ready to say more, but at that moment, we heard some heavy breathing and some stupid moans coming from Chris. Tom smirked, and I watched him carefully crush out his cigarette. Then, with a long sigh, I opened Chris's cooler and found a bag of white, puffy marshmallows. I ate a few and then passed the bag to Tom.

"You know," Tom said, nodding his head while tasting the marshmallows, "I think it all comes back to God. It's all about sin, Apple Jelly. And, from what I've always heard, the wages of sin are death..."

I nodded and almost said, "I'm serious," but stopped, figuring Tom would criticize me again.

"And why it didn't happen is beyond me," Tom said, drifting into thought while munching on another marshmallow. "There she stood, in perfect, ripe beauty, wrapped in comfy, black cotton. At the bottom of the hill, her little, white shoes stuck in the mud, sinking beneath the gray, wet dirt. The wind rippled her wavy, dark hair. The sun brightly pierced her chestnut-brown eyes. And, now, every time I close my eyes..."

"Yeah..."

"I see Maria," Tom said dreamily. "I don't understand it. I mean, I believe there are many loves for everyone: some good, some not so good. With Maria... I don't know. I just know how I feel when I see this girl, even though I don't really know her. Maybe I'm not so much in love with her as I'm in love with who I think she is."

I yawned.

"You know what I mean?" Tom said.

"Hmm?"

"You ever been in love?" Tom asked me.

"Oh, you're right about that," I said.

"What is it with you, Apple Jelly?"

"Huh?" I asked.

"You're not even listening to me," Tom said.

"Oh, I'm sorry."

"Yeah, right," Tom said. "You don't even care."

"Yes, I do," I pleaded. "Just say it again."

"No," Tom said. "If you don't care, then tell me. Don't just sit there eating marshmallows and hiding behind your clean-clothed, pastry-dusted layer of tact. Just spit in my face. But don't give me your transparent fake approval."

I sighed.

"And why do I even need tact?" Tom started up again. "Tact

54

is the first sign of a hypocrite. If you've got something to say, then shout it out. Saving it all until just the right words come out is a lie."

To that, I said nothing; Tom's words made me cringe. Our conversation ended, and there was simply silence: a blankness broken only by the squawks of the "stork" and the mumbles of Chris's voice in the woods.

"Hey!" Tom said, finally perking up. "Why don't we go over and sneak up on 'em?"

"Oh, no…"

"But I'm your captain," Tom said, somewhat playfully. "It's time to cruise."

"Oh, come on, Tom. You can't just go over there."

"But I have to," Tom said. "Look at that sky. It's time to complain about the rain."

"Oh, whatever," I said. "But I know I am not going over there."

Tom stood up and lit another cigarette. "Just hold on," he told me then walked away with a fistful of marshmallows.

CHAPTER 12

Almost immediately, I changed my mind. You see, I know I told Tom I was not going over to see what Chris and Justine were doing—but I couldn't resist. I just could not stay still. So, very carefully, I crept into the pines and moved in just far enough so that I could stay hidden, yet still hear every word.

From my vantage point, Tom appeared to creep up on Chris and Justine, then tower over them like a tall building. Cupping that fistful of marshmallows to his mouth, Tom lifted his right leg and jabbed his foot down on the log a few feet from the couple.

"Just what?" Tom said. "What are you doing over here?"

"What is it you want?" Chris hollered.

"What are you doing?" Tom said.

"Flexing," Chris said. "I'm showing Justy my biceps."

"You're flexing your muscles?" Tom said slowly, like maybe he could not believe what he was saying. "We stopped for all this time so that you could flex your muscles?"

Chris scrambled to his feet and stood bare-chested among the towering pine trees. He held out his right hand, palm up, and demanded, "Why did you come over and bother us?"

"I don't know," Tom said, staring Chris in the eye. "I guess I'm impatient. But just keep on flexing, and I'll give you my cigarette when you finish. It'll be the perfect touch."

Chris grabbed Tom's cigarette from his right hand and slammed it down on the dry pine straw. "I don't want it!" Chris yelled, somewhat out of breath.

Tom stepped back a bit, not saying a word. And that's when I moved back, too. Actually, I retreated all the way to where Tom and I had been sitting with the cooler.

"What is that you're eating?" Chris shouted.

"Oh," Tom said. "It's just a marshmallow."

"You're eating the marshmallows?" Chris hollered fervently as I looked back to see him.

Still without a shirt, bare-chested Chris stepped increasingly closer towards me to yell, "Did I say that you could eat the marshmallows?"

Tom didn't say anything. I didn't, either.

"Lemme tell you a thing or two about those marshmallows," Chris went on. "I brought those marshmallows for me and Jimmy and—for all of us. Like, we were gonna share them. I didn't bring them just so you guys could eat 'em up."

"Well, Jim's not here to eat them," Tom said, sounding funny, but in a cool-jerk way.

"I know that," Chris said. "Jimmy's still in the trailer."

"So, I guess we should have waited for Jim," Tom said.

"And me and Justy," Chris pointed out. "You should have waited for me and Justy."

"But y'all were busy," Tom said.

Chris didn't say anything for a few seconds, but he did keep walking. In fact, Tom and half-naked Chris both kept walking until they were all the way over to me and the cooler.

"Are there any marshmallows left?" Chris yelled.

"I don't know," Tom said, handing Chris the cooler.

Chris opened the red-and-white cooler and found two marshmallows: the ones we had dropped on the ground and ditched because they were dirty. I kind of laughed when Chris wasted no time stuffing that pair of yuckies down his throat.

"Oh, Chris, please," Tom teased, "can't you dress before coming to dinner?"

"Why don't you shut up!" Chris snarled. "You two guys are just lucky I don't have my baseball bat out here or I would crown you."

"Crown me? What, are we playing checkers?" Tom said. "It was just a bunch of marshmallows."

"But they were *my* marshmallows!" Chris shouted.

Right then, I laughed. But really, anyone who would have seen a tall, half-naked, hairy moron standing in a swamp and yelling about marshmallows would have lost it with laughter, too.

CHAPTER 13

Justine didn't say anything: not about Chris, Tom, me, or the marshmallows. In fact, by the time we got back to get Justine, about five minutes after Chris started yelling, she looked like she was asleep next to that half-rotten log.

Tom put his hand on Justine's chest.

"Stop touching her," Chris ordered.

But Tom kept on touching, like he was looking for something.

"Uh-oh," Tom said solemnly.

"What?" Chris shouted.

"I dunno," Tom said then froze as we heard something strange. It almost sounded like those Sss sounds that Tom and Chris were making back on the other side of the swamp, when I told them I was afraid of snakes.

Then, about twelve feet away, we saw what I had feared: a big, nasty-looking snake squirming out of the damp, moldy soil at the base of that half-rotten log.

I shrieked and ran a few yards, tingling with fright.

"What was that?" Tom said quickly.

"Snake!" I shouted. "Snake!"

"What kind?" Tom said.

"It was crawling," I said.

"Was it like, black or green? Or brown?" Tom said.

I danced around in a panic, holding my hands to my mouth and hopping. "It was a snake, Tom, a snake! What does it matter? Let's just go!" I shouted.

"It does matter," Tom said. "And it really matters to Justine."

"Why?" Chris said.

"Well, if it was black, it may not have been anything. And if it was green, it was probably harmless," Tom said. "But if it was brown and had stripes or dots or lines or something, it could be poisonous."

"Poisonous?" I panicked. "Poisonous? Oh, no! Where is it?"

"It took off," Tom said. "It crawled the other way, pretty far, when you went running."

"I thought you said it was too cold for snakes," I said. "Tom! That's what you said!"

"Well, maybe that one was under this log," Tom said. "And I guess it woke up with all of us yelling."

"I didn't never see it," Chris said.

"Did Justine?" Tom asked.

"I don't know," Chris said.

"She looked asleep when I first came over here," Tom said. "She didn't say anything."

"She was relaxing, Tommy. I told you we wanted to relax," Chris said.

"Well, was she asleep?" Tom said.

"She might have been," Chris said.

Shaking his head, Tom leaned down towards Justine with his right ear towards her. "There's nothing," Tom mumbled.

"What do you mean?" Chris said.

Tom let out a long sigh and said, "I think she's done."

"Done?" Chris said.

"She's dead," Tom said softly.

"She's sleeping," Chris insisted.

"She's done," Tom said.

"I can't believe this," I said. "Stupid swamp!"

"Ah, what's the matter with you?" Tom turned around and yelled at me.

"What's wrong with Justy?" Chris shouted. "How do you know what's wrong?"

"Well, I ain't a doctor," Tom said. "But it looks like she was bit by that snake. She ain't waking up."

"What if I kissed her?" Chris said. "What if I did the mouth to mouth?"

"Kissing?" I asked.

"No, it would be kissing to save her," Chris said. "Like the fairy princess. You kiss her, and she's supposed to wake up."

"Like a movie?" I said.

"No, not like a movie," Chris said. "It's the real thing. The mouth to mouth. Here..."

Chris stopped talking and leaned down, still bare-chested. He grabbed Justine's shoulders and kissed her. But he looked like he was trying to be romantic. I mean, this didn't look like any mouth to mouth to me. It just looked like kissing. And it seemed dumb, too, since that was kind of how all this got started in the first place—with that leech begging her for a kiss, even before we got off the boat.

"Lemme do it," Tom said. "You ain't doing nothing but kissing her. You're supposed to hold her nose, breathe in her mouth, and tap her stomach with your hands, and try to get her breath and heart all started again."

"No," Chris said. "You cannot. You are in love with her."

"Either that or you'll give her cancer," I said to Tom. "It doesn't matter if she was bit by a snake or not. Having you do it is just going to give her cancer from your cigarettes."

Tom gave me a dirty look. Then he turned away with a huff.

Chris and I never let our eyes leave Justine. Suddenly, though, Chris turned to look at me and put his hand on my shoulder.

"You do it," Chris said. "Please," Chris begged, standing tall with a tear streaming down his cheek.

I did not know what to say nor did I know what to do. I didn't want to kiss Justine; I knew that. I didn't want to do what Chris called "the mouth to mouth," either. But Chris would not stop crying.

"Please," he said again.

"Oh, I do not believe this!" I said with a sigh of frustration. Then I dropped to my knees and closed my eyes. I took a deep breath and faintly smelled smoke. I did not look, but I guessed Tom was at it again with another cigarette.

My shoulders and head sank lower and lower, until I felt Justine's lips meet mine. I didn't know what to do. I mean, I thought I was supposed to kiss her, but her lips felt motionless—good, but motionless.

Why? I thought. *Why does my first kiss happen in a swamp, trying to save some girl I hardly know?*

I pulled away and looked up to see Tom. "I don't know what I'm doing," I told him. "How does this help?"

"I'll do it," Tom said brashly.

"No, you won't," Chris said. "You're just going to kiss her. I want you to save her."

"She wouldn't even be in this mess if we had just kept walking instead of you running over here to flex your muscles," Tom said to Chris.

"No," Chris shouted. "You should have kept out of my cooler. All Justy was doing was relaxing."

Tom did not say anything. He just turned and started the mouth to mouth on Justine. And that was really weird. Seeing Tom kiss Justine was like watching the third round of spin-the-bottle, swamp-style. It just didn't seem right.

Only, Tom really did not look like he was kissing Justine at all. He actually looked like he knew what he was doing, except I don't know how he did. He probably saw mouth to mouth in a movie or something. He was no doctor. I mean, how could he be a doctor when he smoked cigarettes? How can anybody be a doctor and smoke cigarettes, knowing that the cigarettes are going to kill their patients and probably kill them, too?

Over and over, Tom pushed on Justine's tummy and then kissed her, giving her the mouth to mouth, as he called it, and then tried to see if anything was working.

Chris appeared to panic.

I didn't say anything. But I gulped, knowing the inevitable announcement to come after a tired Tom finally leaned up after a couple minutes of trying mouth to mouth.

"She's dead," Tom said quietly.

"Dead?" I said.

"Maybe she's in a coda," Chris suggested.

"A *coma?*" I asked. "Or how do we know she's really dead?"

"I'm serious," Tom said, but not like he was mocking me.

Silence came between us.

"She's dead," Tom said. "And if you don't want to die, you'd better get out of here, too."

Chris fell backwards, landing on the pine straw, his long arms dropping. His hairy, half-nude frame sprawled in a crucifix position. "I killed you!" he babbled through tears.

"Shut up!" Tom shouted and kicked Chris's arm.

I took a deep sigh and smelled a whiff of smoke in the air as Tom kept kicking Chris and yelling at him. Chris finally got to his feet, and I figured he would want to brawl. But he did not. Chris just put his shirt back on as Tom howled at him to "Get out!"

That's when Tom took off running, out of the pines and back to the marsh.

"Let's go! Let's go!" Tom shouted.

Chris kept on crying, mumbling something about Justine, as

we both got up and chased after Tom.

 We'll dwell here forever, I thought: *We'll be like Justine, dying in a place where there are no rules.*

CHAPTER 14

I have always heard there was supposed to be mourning when someone died. Yet Tom shed no tears, did not even pause. He just ripped through the marsh and blazed a tyrant's trail so fast that it seemed like he was the one who had killed Justine.

A marsh stalk slapped me in the face. I stepped in one mud-hole after another, and every hole I squished into seemed like a prime spot for a snake. Maybe that was why we were running; maybe Tom thought the whole swamp was full of snakes. That made sense to me. But Tom would not tell us. He also did not tell us why we didn't try to carry Justine away. He didn't tell us anything, actually.

Then, feeling so overwhelmed that I couldn't hold back for anything or anybody, I exploded with a shout. "How come we did not take her body?"

"Because we can't!" Tom returned.

"I wanna go back!" Chris cried.

Tom ignored Chris and ran even faster through the six-foot-tall marsh stalks.

"I think he's hiding something," I said to Chris, trying to be quiet so that Tom would not hear me. "Maybe it has something to do with the smoke."

"What smoke?" Chris said.

I shrunk back, thinking that only I had seen the smoke. But at the same time, I also kept running, with Chris running behind me and bouncing along with gargled mumbles that I could not understand.

"I'm not going on anymore," Chris suddenly yelled in a whiny voice. "I gotta go back to Justy!"

"Tom!" I hollered with desperation.

This is it, I thought. *That great, proverbial point of everybody losing it.*

"What do you want?" Tom asked, suddenly stopping his stride.

"We have to stop and talk about all this," I said. "You're acting like a tyrant."

"Oh, really?" Tom asked, sounding bitter. "You wanna have a grief counseling session for the wimpy suburban boys?"

"We need to talk!" I shouted.

"About what?" Tom shot back. "About our emotions? Oh, yeah...and how you don't call any of us your friend."

"That's not it!" I shouted.

"Well, whaddaya think the American settlers did when somebody died?" Tom said. "You think they sat around crying about it in a swamp?"

"Tom, at least we could go back and bury her," I said.

"I wanna know what happened!" Chris cried.

"A snake bit her," Tom said. "And if you don't wanna die, then you better keep going before one bites you."

Again, Tom took off running across the muddy, messy ground. I ran, too, but Chris stayed put.

"You have to help Chris," I said as I ran. "He's not well."

"I don't have to do anything," Tom said, not turning around. "And you don't even like Chris."

"He's losing it," I said.

"Like you care," Tom said. "You guys wanted to make this swamp a free-living, play-around zoo."

Saying that made me mad: I wanted to tell Tom how he was wrong, especially since I never wanted Chris and Justine to "relax." But Chris interrupted me, standing a few feet behind us.

"I wanna know what happened!" Chris cried again.

Tom turned and walked back towards Chris. "I dunno," Tom said, this time actually sounding nice. "But it seems like you never get answers when something you care about gets taken away."

Chris looked at Tom and said, "I wanna go back."

"She's done," Tom said.

"How do you know?" Chris said, suddenly sounding forceful. "How do you know that?"

"Subject change! Subject change!" I shouted.

Tom made a quick turn-about towards me and said, "What is it with you, Apple Jelly? You got a grammar lesson leaking out of your head?"

"No," I said. "But either we change the subject, or we sit down right now and talk about how we can work all this out. I think you will both agree that the last half-hour has been quite the trying experience."

"Man, shut up," Tom said.

"Oh, what do you want to do?" I asked. "You want everyone to be as bitter as you?"

"Shut *up*!" Tom ordered.

"I want some answers," I declared. "I want to know why you keep hiding from this, Tom. Your kind of numbness will only eat at you. It'll shrink you to nothing, I swear."

Tom slapped his forehead with a vicious laugh and bounced a couple hops across the marsh. "You change your mind every second," he said. "You're lobbying back there to change the subject. And now you're howling that you want some answers, meaning let's crank up your naive, teenage, soul-searching eulogy—and that, I'm telling you, is something we ain't got time for. We ain't gonna do it."

67

"You have got a lot of problems," I said to Tom.

"Watch your mouth," Tom said.

"Do you even know what your problem is?" I asked Tom.

"Tell me," Tom said. "For the third time today, tell me what my problem is."

"You think that just because we're a bunch of stupid, naive teenagers who don't understand the world then we should all shut up and not say anything until we do have all the answers."

"Well, don't you?" Tom said. "You're the fool who can't even spring a leak in the woods and whose main goal in life is to never be embarrassed. Wouldn't some naive assumption make you feel young and stupid?"

"Maybe," I said, "but what does that mean?"

Tom turned and started walking again.

By then, my brain was so cluttered with crap that all I knew to do was walk behind and follow. Silence came between us, and, with that silence, Tom gradually started going faster.

"I'm—tired," I said between heavy pants.

"That comes from wasting time," Tom snarled and tore off like he was trying to lose me.

Left and right, marsh stalks slapped me in the face as I struggled to keep up with Tom's pace. "Maybe the wages of sin are death. And maybe the snake coming in was part of the original sin," I mumbled to myself.

"All these thorns," I said with a louder tone, not actually knowing now how loud I spoke. "This must be what Adam and Eve went through."

"The apple!" Tom shouted. "The apple!"

"What did I do?" I asked.

"The marshmallows!" Tom shouted. "The marshmallows!"

"Huh?" I said.

Tom did not answer. He just kept running doggedly, and I simply continued to follow. Before I knew it, a few steps had turned into many, so many that there was no way to count. I just kept walking, not knowing where I was going and not really willing to care. Blindly, I just kept moving under that gray cloud.

CHAPTER 15

W here's Chris?" Tom said, coming to a stop a couple of minutes later.

I turned around. I didn't have much room to turn, but I did,
clumsily, then stood on my tip-toes and peered across the field,
looking over the six-foot-high, waving reeds.

I saw the pines first, and then I saw the smoke.

"What is that?" Tom asked me, looking back at the pines.

It was strangely comforting to know someone else had seen
the smoke.

"Was that—"

"I saw the smoke before," I said. "And oh, no. I think it's—"

"Where's Chris?"

I didn't answer. Like me, Tom must have known where Chris
had gone. As for the smoke, though, it finally dawned on me what
that must have been: Tom's messy habit of cigarette smoking.

Tom may have looked tough, like he could handle smoke going in and out of his body. But when he played with fire, I found
myself watching his every move. Still, back in the pines, I couldn't
be so careful. I had been hiding to eavesdrop on Tom, Chris, and
Justine. I didn't get the chance to check what happened to Tom's
cigarette.

Now, there was no raging forest fire. But you could see and

smell smoke. It was spooky, too, coming from where everything had changed with the snake and Justine, the marshmallows and Chris.

Tom started moving forward again but much more moderately, almost like this was now a nature walk.

I looked ahead and did not dare turn around.

"The smoke is death," Tom said. "That's all we see."

To that, I did not reply. Tom's statement was philosophical to the point of being ridiculous; that smoke was simply Tom's cigarette.

Tom must be losing it, I thought. *Maybe falling overboard caused him to develop a fever.*

We walked a few more steps until Tom stood motionless, looking across a great field of brown and green. "You know," he said, "this really isn't even a swamp. It's just some marsh and reeds."

Tom started walking again but now with even slower steps as we came into clear view of the tributary creek Tom had mentioned earlier. But that stream, I could tell, was not all that occupied Tom's mind.

"Does it really matter what we call it?" I mumbled.

"It doesn't matter to you," Tom said distantly, his eyes focused on the creek. "Or does it?" he asked, suddenly turning my way. "What is this? What is this place?"

"A marsh field," I said, trying for an answer.

"What is it?" Tom asked again.

"A pile of weeds...uh, a muddy creek-bed with yellow reeds..."

"C'mon! What is it?"

"It's... I don't know. A pile of weeds?"

"Apple Jelly!" Tom shouted. "Don't ask me what it is. Tell me what it is. Don't just look at the surface, Apple Jelly. All you ever see is the surface!"

"Oh, now, Tom, it's going to be OK," I said, grabbing his arm and wondering seriously why we were talking this way.

"No, it will not all be OK! Tom said and pulled away. "You'll just keep drifting, Apple Jelly."

Tom stopped near the creek bank and held out his arms. "This is more than just marsh reeds," he said. "This is life's gritty and muddy struggle to see the end."

"Oh, come on, Tom. Stop talking like that. Remember, we've got to get home."

"Why?" he said crazily. "Just tell me why!"

I didn't know what to say.

"Why do we always run away from the open ground?" Tom asked.

I gave Tom a strange look but said nothing.

"Here," Tom said. "Here, we could have the perfect peace Emerson and Thoreau always wanted. Cast off your environment! You're not in anyone's society but yours and mine."

Oh, no, I thought. *Here he goes with that school stuff again.*

I grabbed Tom's arm and told him again that we had to get home. But when I did, Tom pulled his arm away. For a long spell, he just stared at me.

Tom is really losing it, I thought.

"Doesn't it bother you the way society has scraped your mind?" Tom asked me. "Do you actually need TV sitcoms and shopping malls? Do you? No! You only need to find yourself by yourself. Here, in this swamp, we can do that—in a place where the land is free and the life is free."

"The life is free?"

"Every bit of it," Tom said, nodding. "Outside, that's where it all costs."

"But look at all the troubles this place has already cost us."

"Troubles? Here? No way," Tom said. "Nature deals us just what we deserve. Outside, that's the rot. That's the cheats and the deceptions and some jerk with a beard going after your wife."

Tom shook his head and sat down at the creek bank. "We don't need it," he said. "We could pretend... No, we could absolutely forget we were ever part of that society."

"Oh, come on, Tom. Just stand up. You're dreaming or something. We have to go."

"No, we don't!" Tom shouted, pulling away from me. "What is it with you, Apple Jelly? Why do we want to run out of here as fast as we can?"

I sighed and tried an offensive approach: "Because you were the one telling us to run!" I said.

"Well, maybe I was wrong," Tom said quietly. He stood up and threw a clump of dirt in the creek. For a minute, we both just watched the water ripple.

I gripped Tom's arm. "This way?" I said, pointing to a skinny duck trail along the bank of the creek.

"Any way, I suppose," Tom replied. "We just have to keep walking."

"That's right," I said. "We have to find our way home."

"Or at least the rest of it," Tom said.

CHAPTER 16

Wind gusts increased, making me cold, a feeling which, in turn, made me remember our lack of a bathroom.

"I suppose we need rules," Tom said while slowly walking. "Without them, we'd just kill each other. One of us might bake the bread, but who would actually eat it?"

"We would share it," I said.

"No, we wouldn't. We'd kill each other for it."

"No, we would share it. Just like the marshmallows. I know we would."

Tom shook his head. He stopped walking and said, "Take off your mask, Apple Jelly. Admit it; you'd kill me."

"No, I would not. Stop saying that."

Tom turned and walked on, still going slow. "Someday, Apple Jelly," he said. "Someday you'll leak so much truth out of yourself you'll feel like a fool for having held it in for so long."

I didn't say anything. And, for the next couple of minutes, we did not exchange a single word.

Step by step, we followed the banks of the stream Tom called Purgatory Creek. I turned back—Tom never did, not even once—and saw the smoke cloud. It made me feel guilty, too, especially when the smell hit my nose in the breeze, and I was unable to shake the scent that Tom called "death." That smell made me wonder how that snake killed Justine, and it made me wonder what happened to Chris. Was he trying to save Justine, or was he dead, too? It made me question whether we should keep walking to get out and get help, or should we just turn around and try to find Chris? I felt like shouting Chris's name, but I did not. I just kept walking, selfishly it seemed, as another part of me said we would never find Chris even if we went back, and we would probably end up killing ourselves in the process.

Trying to distance my mind from that dilemma, I looked out to the open side of the trail, away from the creek. "You know," I said without really knowing what I was saying, "I'll bet this place is big enough for a mall."

"Is that what you're thinking?" Tom said casually.

"Well, it is," I said.

"I don't believe you! You'd really want to spoil what we have here by building a stupid shopping mall?"

"Well, it would be nice," I said.

"Is that the driving force in your rush back to society? To get to the mall?"

I giggled. With all that had happened, though, I thought laughter would be good medicine. "Well," I said, "the mall and a bathroom. That would be cool by me."

"I don't believe you!" Tom snapped. "Do you even know what's the best thing out here? The fact that you can't even see a mall!"

"Ah!" I let out, suddenly feeling as scraped raw as anything. "Rant and rave! That's all you ever do! All you ever want to do is be a freak. You put down everything. Why? Tell me! *Why* do you always carry on like you do?"

"Because I want to be awake," Tom said. "I'm tired of being in a teen-age cloud of not seeing how things really are."

"Uh-huh," I said. "And what makes you think you're old enough to know how things really are?"

"Well, I'm sixteen. Just like you. Now is the time to cast off the puffy, sugary security of stupidity and find all the answers."

"Uh-huh," I said.

"And hey, I know I'll never have all the answers," Tom said, "but I still want to find them."

"Uh-huh," I said again. "Tom...uh, I wasn't going to tell you this, but, well, I think I have to. You see, your shell is cracked. And I swear it's only a matter of time before your egg runs out and somebody fries it on the concrete."

"The concrete?" Tom said. "Why the concrete?"

"Huh?"

"You're drooling for it, aren't you?" Tom said. "You have to have the roots, the foundations, the concrete. You're afraid of having all this freedom."

I didn't say anything. I looked at Tom, but I did not say a word.

Silence fell between us again as we continued to walk.

I still thought Tom was crazy. But at the same time, I could see some truth in what he said. I needed concrete beneath my shoes. I needed to be regulated by society. I needed to follow a schedule, eat just about the same thing every day, and think about going to college and finding a job and buying a house and all that stuff you're supposed to do. It made sense. My only problem was that I didn't know whether to feel satisfied or sorrowful about all that.

A minute later, I asked Tom when he "woke up."

"Here," he said. "It was here when I saw how guilty I was. I could tell I was already rotting..."

Tom paused then added, "And we always had to go there, didn't we?"

"Go where?"

"The mall," Tom said. "Typical teens. Going to the mall was our social homework. It was pointless, too. Just as pointless as this swamp hike, if you think about it. I mean, all we ever do is walk and walk and walk. Why? And to where? For what?"

"We go there for security," I guessed. "There are walls at the mall."

"Walls?" Tom said. "Yeah, that has to be it. It keeps everybody in, keeps everybody sheltered. It's another part of that teen thing. It's keeping everybody inside that social-circle life cycle. You keep yourself and everybody else so tightly wound you can't decide whether to eat lunch without hearing three opinions besides your own."

"I'm serious."

"But maybe teenagers don't know anything more than collecting favorable opinions from their friends," Tom continued. "They're all in that endless sea of shampoo and skating rinks, drifting from block to block in their little cars, ready to gag or laugh at whatever mass product society spits at them. And none of it has to do with taste. It's like some kind of half sleep, or something. Just sixteen years of blocking out the bad and the indecipherable—"

"And getting stuck in the concrete," I said with a giggle, speaking almost subconsciously.

"Yep," Tom said. "Without it, we're all just in the woods. And for the sake of the children, we can't have that. No, sir, they won't let us."

"They?" I said, trying to sound funny. "Who is they?"

"The mainstream people: The Society to Control the Opinion of the Public."

CHAPTER 17

The walk continued; the talk did not. Tom said, "I should be shot," but then said no more.

In the silence, I retreated into my own thoughts—muddled, initially, but then clearing, much like my face after a good scrubbing.

Alone practically, moving several steps behind Tom, I found everything along the trail seemed like a childhood experience. My mind caught awe in hearing the squawks of seagulls and quacks of the ducks.

Together, Tom and I continued along the banks of Purgatory Creek. It felt strangely taboo when Tom silently lit a cigarette; the fire seemed to shatter some sort of innocence. The whole idea of smoking resembled the wild brush on our sides: Touching the brush was tempting, but it could be sharp and painful if you did not quickly pull away.

Smoking that cigarette—that's where it all started changing. Just finding the right path proved to be near impossible.

From our trusted trail, I saw small openings leading to the uninhabited and uninhibited wild side: areas that instinct told me to avoid. Soon, there were so many cottonwood branches blocking our trail that we had to break them just to find a space to walk. Our trusted trail along the creek would ultimately vanish. Bothersome branches got in the way, and, at times, I wondered if fighting through all the claws and thorns was worth it.

Nature doesn't play fair, I thought. *We have been cheated, our pathway stolen.* Losing the trail reminded me of snow that does not pack, or a sunny day that turns cloudy.

It seems we never get answers when something we trust gets taken away.

I heard distant thunder, and I winced at its angry noise. It sounded like we were being scolded just for trying to find our way through the world. But it wasn't the thunder that ended my daydream, it was seeing something civilized standing near the banks of Purgatory Creek. It appeared so out of place that it seemed invasive; a wooden duck blind with three-foot-high walls, built around a slab of concrete. The sight made Tom cough, then gag, then fall to his knees, tenaciously clinging to its walls.

Until that moment, in my innocence, I had imagined the path Tom and I had been following was made by wild animals. But this proved that we really weren't the first ones to find Purgatory Creek.

"Lord!" Tom cried, kneeling and raising his arms.

Tom's behavior seemed overly dramatic, and I certainly was not to the point of matching his mercurial mood. But still, I felt "scraped," as Tom would put it. *No place and no peace is safe and sacred. Sooner or later, it all gets shattered*, I thought.

Slowly, Tom crawled inside the three walls of the duck blind. His back fell against the wall opposite the opening, and his legs stretched across some marsh stalks covering the concrete.

An odd grin passed over Tom's face as he pointed to the thin ring of smoke rising out of the pines. "I think they're dead," he said.

I felt too frightened to reply.

"So, what have you been doing?" Tom said strangely. "I've been killing people all day."

I did not say anything. I just watched as Tom banged the back of his head against one wall of the duck blind. Then he looked up into the dark clouds and pulled apart a piece of marsh straw.

"Justine saved me when I couldn't go on," Tom said. "And then, when it was my turn, I just gave up and ran."

"What?" I asked him. "I thought you said Justine was dead."

Tom hung his head. "I don't know," he said, lifting his face. His eyes were glassed over with tears when he added, "I don't know what dead people look like."

I didn't say anything. But this was a light-bulb moment if there ever was one, making me seriously wonder why I had followed Tom instead of turning back to find Chris.

"So full of life, that little anarchist, to be brought down by a tyrant," Tom mumbled. "She went out on a log, Apple Jelly. She died for a cause."

"What?" I said, knowing Tom's shell was cracked for sure. "She was bit by a snake. That's what you told us. You were so sure of that. What do you mean, 'dying for a cause'?"

"She did," Tom said, facing the distance. "She saw anarchy as her only way out, and she knew what had to be done. She didn't blindly drift."

"What are you talking about? What do you mean 'blindly drift'? She had a thing for Chris, didn't she? That's certainly drifting into something."

"But it was all part of her plan," Tom explained, like he was in a haze. "She saw the tyranny that would have to come to lead us this far. She knew that she could never survive in that world. She needed no rules."

I heard all this from Tom, but I really did not know how to understand it. Tom's weird words seemed other-worldly; it was not only what Tom said, but how he said it.

"She saved me," Tom said, sounding so sure of himself.

Hearing that, I wondered what was really inside Tom's cracked shell: a raw egg or a live animal.

"Maybe Chris is back there trying to save her," I suggested.

Tom looked up at me. Then he returned to his haze, shaking

his head.

"Should we shout for him?" I said.

"Sure," Tom said. "Cry in vain."

"Chris!" I screamed. "Chris!"

Tom just looked at me, blankly.

"Chris!" I shouted a third time, nearly sweating with anticipation.

It was as silent as could be, though. I heard the sound of absolutely nothing.

"She saved me," Tom mumbled.

To that, I had no reply.

"If it wasn't for Justine saving my spirit when I collapsed, I would have dug my own grave," Tom said. "It was like she knew how things would have to be. She was a visionary, Apple Jelly: a poetic dreamer higher than life."

Tom made eye contact with me, and I'm sure my face must have simply looked bored. I tried to follow what Tom was saying, but I just couldn't. I simply sighed. And, with that sigh, it was clear my patience of listening to Tom ramble freely had run its course.

"You know," I said with a smile, "I'll bet this is the longest I've ever talked to you with the same shirt on."

"*Is that all you ever think about?!*" Tom exploded.

"No," I replied softly.

"You fashionized idiot!" Tom howled and hopped to his feet on the concrete. "Tell me, does that shirt make you who you are?"

"I don't know," I said. "I mean, I have always heard 'Clothes make the man.'"

"That's what you've heard," Tom said. "But is that what you think?"

"Huh?"

"Give me your shirt," Tom demanded.

"No."

"Apple Jelly," Tom said, trying to sound nice. "Just give me your shirt."

"Why?"

"Because," he said, "I want to prove something."

"What's that?" I snapped.

"You aren't what you wear," Tom said and slipped off Chris's leather jacket. He then helped me pull off my jacket and shirt, and he told me to slip on Chris's jacket.

It's too cold to play these games, I thought.

"Now," Tom said, "are you still the same?"

"Yes."

"Why?" Tom said.

"I don't know. You tell me, smarty."

"Clothes are just the outer shell. Don't you remember reading Thoreau?" Tom asked me.

I didn't answer. Honestly, Tom's Thoreau thing grated on my nerves. I mean, by that point, I had just totally had it with Tom's school stuff. All I really wanted to know by then was what had happened to Chris and Justine.

Tom gave me back my clothes, and he fell back against one wall of the duck blind. "Since this is already here," he said in a calm tone, "then there's no sense building elsewhere."

"Building what?" I said. "Wait—are you still serious about living out here?"

Tom just looked at me.

"Have you lost your mind?" I asked. "Don't you have any idea how stupid it is to want to live in a swamp?"

Tom did not answer at first. But then he started to smile. "Here," he said, "I can write and sing."

"Write what? Poetry?" I said, somewhat sarcastically.

"Yeah, a little," Tom replied. "What I want to do is write a book."

"Another *Walden* or something? You want to write another *Walden*? Oh, Tom, you *are* crazy," I said. "Thinking you'll live out here... That by itself is foolish."

"To who? You? I don't care if living here isn't so-called real-world practical," Tom said. "I just know I have to stay here."

I sighed.

"Here is where I can fix it," Tom went on, like he was trying to convince me. "I can hold on to all the broken dreams we give up when we stop dreaming."

"And you think you'll make money writing some dreamers' handbook?" I asked.

Shaking his head, Tom said, "Doing it all for money would be equal to a blank tale of nothing."

Tom turned and rested his elbow atop one wall of the duck blind. Staring at the waters of Purgatory Creek, he said, "I would write a book much like this place. It would be open and free to explore anything from one page to the next. The plot might be like a meandering stream. The theme would be the sediment. And there, in that stream, nothing would ever get clogged, and nobody would blindly drift."

Silence came between us, and I locked myself into Tom's words.

"Nobody would blindly drift," I said, finally trying to understand what he meant.

Tom nodded, still staring into the water.

"But, like, what if somebody drowned?"

At that, Tom's face turned to stone. His eyes became hazy and tearful. And as much as I wanted to say "I'm sorry," I was too afraid to say or do anything more. I simply stared at Tom as he sat there, swamped with emotions. Fact is, I needed Tom to get up and tell me what to do next. But he did nothing. One minute turned to many on that slab of concrete, leaving me feeling completely stuck.

CHAPTER 18

Decisively, I turned away from Tom. It was tough, and it felt both right and wrong. But I knew I could no longer handle the haze in Tom's eyes; he was in a daze for which I could apparently do nothing, and which I may have caused.

At that point, I do not even know that I cared about Tom. I mean, he was my friend— my school friend—but what use was he to me in that condition?

I walked backwards, my heart racing and my palms sweating, worried I was making all the wrong moves, especially when I looked up at those dark clouds and realized I had no idea what I was doing.

"Going backwards," I said. "This is the dumbest thing I have ever done."

But it was just time to go; Tom was a dead-end. That's all I could think as one step turned to another.

I first pushed my way back through that tough thicket and then regained my footing on the duck trail along Purgatory Creek. From there, I could clearly see the pines, and I began to run, figuring I could outpace the snakes.

Chris! Of all people, I could not believe I was running to find Chris!

What was weird is that I was surprised by how fast I could

move. It seems that Tom and I had stopped and started so much that we had hardly gotten anywhere. Yes, it made sense when I asked to stop and talk about what had happened to Justine, but what about all of Tom's poetic nonsense? I mean, whatever happened to just wrecking a boat and walking back to civilization?

In no time, it seemed, I was off the trail and running back through the tall marsh. And you know what? It was easy. I didn't need a leader; maybe all I really needed was me.

"Chris!" I shouted.

But I ran too fast to wait for a reply.

Feeling out of breath, I found my feet again at the edge of the pines, edging closer to the spot where Tom and I ate the marshmallows. There, I found Chris's red-and-white cooler still sitting where we had forgotten it. I flipped open the lid. Beneath the bag of marshmallows, I found an empty container of Benadryl, the kind of allergy medicine that always made my mom very sleepy.

I sat with the cooler for a minute, wondering why I hadn't noticed that medicine earlier. I also wondered why I had been so dumb as to go back to the pines, and not just kick Tom the way Tom had kicked Chris, then told him to start moving and to run.

Instead, I suddenly kicked myself. I got up and crept further into the pines, first finding my eavesdropping position, then running wildly towards that half-rotten log—although I was worried that I would also see a half-rotten corpse.

Practically in a panic, I breathed heavily and inhaled deeply. In fact, I inhaled so deeply that I suddenly got a whiff of what appeared to be clean air.

Oddly, I didn't suck in smoke. What I breathed smelled more like a fire that had been extinguished. And that's exactly what I found, too, when I reached the log. The fire was gone, but so were Chris and Justine.

The tomb was empty!

CHAPTER 19

I was terrified. None of this made sense. And I was suddenly scared that any move or noise I would make would awaken a snake. So I bolted, running out of the pines and back to the marsh, feeling swamped with confusion.

"Chris!" I shouted.

But I ran too fast to wait for a reply.

Mired in mystery, my mind became flooded with flashbacks. Plain as day, I could see Chris talking to Justine's grandmother—that mean old lady with the afghans. She was looking him up and down like he was trash, and he was acting strangely suspicious about something.

Who was Chris? Was he a saint or a sinner? Did he actually come back to the pines and save Justine? Maybe he gave her more mouth to mouth and they marched off, hand in hand.

In no time, amid all these thoughts, I found I had reached the banks of Purgatory Creek and the skinny duck trail. And that's where my mind entered another daydream, as I followed the same path where, earlier that day, I had imagined the awakening of spring and the state of innocence.

I could see Justine again. She was sneezing as we first took off on the boat, and it was muffled, kind of like a cute kitten sneeze. She giggled, too, and said, "It's my allergies. I may have to pop a pill."

"Pop a pill?" Tom shouted. "I don't want no drugs on this boat."

"It's just medicine," Justine said.

"What about booze?" Chris added with a laugh. "I got something that could make this a booze cruise."

"Booze cruise?" I shouted as I rowed the boat. "Are you talking about alcohol?"

Chris let out a stupid laugh.

"Alcohol is illegal," I said. "We are not old enough. I don't want to get in trouble."

"There ain't no trouble 'less when get caught," Justine said, slyly.

"And these are the high seas!" Tom shouted as he leaned off the bow of the boat. "It all falls to maritime law!"

"Oh, blow!" Justine said as the wind picked up its breeze against the back of the boat.

"Follow me to the sea!" Tom shouted. "Unto the sea we shall be!"

SNAP!

That was it: the pivotal point. That was literally when everything changed, just as Tom made that stupid proclamation. We were blindly drifting away from the camp as one of the boat's oars cracked, and this whole mess began.

"Stupid swamp!" I shouted as my daydream abruptly flipped back to the reality of seeing briars and cottonwoods blocking the duck trail.

"Tom!" I shouted, hearing my voice echo.

But I did not wait for a reply. I madly tugged at a tree, anxious to keep going. I pulled back a branch, and it broke free. Then I raced forward.

Sweat poured down my face. I could not stop panting. I ran all the way to the concrete of the duck blind, and it was all I could do to catch my breath. I wheezed as I scanned the swamp in silence. I felt like a forsaken fool as I watched the sun sink in the western horizon.

Tom was gone. I was totally alone in the darkness.

CHAPTER 20

The clouds burst, finally, and that long-dreaded rain came as I was surrounded by trees dusted with mist. I had gone just a few yards beyond the duck blind but found endless branches of oaks, pines, and maples bashing my brain when I could not see them.

I should have known this walk in the woods must be made alone, and I could do nothing but feel lost. But I guess that's life: You're supposed to feel lost. Maybe you're even supposed to get used to it.

I never needed a walking stick before, but I seized one then simply to have a companion. Perhaps that sturdy piece of wood was like one of Tom's cigarettes; it was my friend. God knows I needed one: All my other friends were gone.

I crazily cried out, hoping to hear Chris's voice again. I also prayed I could find Tom. And though I barely knew her, I yearned to hear Justine carry on about staying out all night: "We're young, and we don't know what's coming, so who cares about getting there?!"

I was lost.

Pour rain, I thought. *Pour rain until it's all blocked out. Each wet, stinking step sinks me deeper in the mud. And I don't even know why I am making these steps. I just know that I have to move to prove that I am not stupid, to keep explaining myself, and then rush back to the concrete where those same, tired questions never cease: "What have you been up to?" or "What have you accomplished?" or "How much money do you make?"*

I never lived for what I thought; I had only lived to answer those questions. On that trail, all alone, I was growing older with each step. I could hear the rain and thunder, the anguish and the anger. The rain was so cold as I ran, breath-heavy, that it nearly made me blind.

The walking stick soon became my cane.

"Ouch!"

I slammed into a tree I could not see. My nose hit a limb as I lost my footing on the soggy ground. It was miserably cold, and the sting of that branch had me shouting again.

"Ouch!"

But who would hear me?

I was drifting blindly until I got stuck on a limb and was afraid to move. I prayed for a moment and then I swore, shaking and sweating. The rain was so cold it felt more like ice. There was no trace of spring. The ice would soon freeze me, I feared, and the harsh rain seemed as if it would never end.

I think I died.

My eyes were closed. Yet, in my mind, I could find the pines. There, I had kissed a girl, and I liked it. She might have even been dead when I did it. And she was kissed by one boy before and one boy after.

Could that have been love?

Perhaps, I thought, *this cold, dark rain is a shower for my soul.* I could still faintly feel some tears on my cheeks. And I longed to see the lightning, up in heaven, slashing the sky with a bolt of blinding beauty.

Decisively, I pulled away, suddenly feeling as scraped as anything. Then, that entire tree limb slapped me in the face.

"Ouch!"

So, yes, I was alive. I was even awake, and I knew that every step would be one that I had to make for myself.

Feeling free, I pulled down my pants and simply let go. So much truth flowed out of me that I felt like a fool for having held it in for so long. Springing a leak gave me sight where there was none in the dark woods chilled by the rain.

It made me remember the need for unbridled, not-afraid-to-be-embarrassed silliness. It made me remember the camp and how Tom gave strange nicknames to everyone he met. A fat, burly, hairy fellow he named "Cycle Jones." "Mow-Mow Pinky" wore pink sunglasses and cut the grass. "Johnnie Arcade" was an all-smiles, know-it-all kid who hung out in the game room. "Miss Little Tide"—or maybe it was "Little Miss Tide"—was the cutest, blonde three-year-old girl in the world; we met her while she carried a huge box of Tide Detergent down the campground road. When Tom said he was going to start calling everybody these nicknames to their face, I told him I wanted no part of it. I don't know if he ever did that or not, but I clearly remembered how uniquely Tom replied to my objections: "What would it matter? You'll never see these people again. None of us will. So what's wrong with being a freak?"

Nothing. In the rain and in the dark, I could see it would not matter.

I remembered how Tom told me he didn't mind looking like a freak if there was a good cause behind it. And, to Tom, calling people silly nicknames was a cause; it was unrestrained, who-cares-about-opinions silliness. We all have a need for that.

CHAPTER 21

The rain slowed its pouring, and I found the flowing waters of Purgatory Creek wrapped around both sides of the trail I had blazed. Looking beyond, in the shadows of the moonlight, I knew I had to make a crossing.

So I took my cane—that twisted branch—and entered the creek's dark, gloomy waters. Its frothy, green murk washed up to my waist as I poked around, looking for safe passage. But I trembled in that water, colder than rain, and the chill made me take a spill. I slipped so far that my head was dunked in the water like a Baptism.

I gasped for air, yelling a little, until I found my feet and coughed. I reached up to grab a handful of vines, belly-crawled atop a dirt mound, then simply stopped. By then, the rain was over, but I could hear left-over raindrops still falling from the trees amid the chirps of crickets.

But that was not all that I heard. A scuffling sound that sounded like a very large animal suddenly made me freeze.

"Where have you been?" I heard a voice whisper.

I didn't answer. I was actually afraid to answer. I knew that whisper did not belong to Tom. No, it sounded like a stranger, which made me paranoid, fearing that this was some police officer or camp official wanting to know what I had done with the boat, Justine, Chris, or Tom.

Afraid I was going to be arrested, I lay flat on the dirt mound, hoping I could make myself invisible.

"Where have you been?" that voice whispered again.

I still did not answer.

"I have been waiting," the voice whispered.

In silence, my mind ran through all the possibilities of who that voice could belong to, but nothing about that whisper made sense.

"Where have you been?" the voice whispered again.

By then, I had my eyes tightly shut and was curled up in a fetal position with one question: Was this God speaking to me?

I had crossed Purgatory Creek and pulled myself up the vines until I landed on that dirt mound. *Am I in heaven?* I wondered.

"I heard you call my name," the voice whispered.

This must be Jesus Christ, I thought. *Purgatory Creek must actually be purgatory.*

"I forgive you," that voice whispered.

"I know I don't deserve to be here," I managed to whimper.

"To be where?" the voice whispered.

"In heaven," I said softly.

"This is not heaven," the voice whispered.

Hearing that, I got cold chills and had more questions. *Where had I landed? Where was this dirt mound? If I went through purgatory, and if this was not heaven, then it could only be...*

"This is not heaven," the voice whispered again.

"This is not heaven?" I somehow had the courage to ask.

The voice did not respond.

"This is not heaven?" I asked again, speaking louder.

The voice still did not respond.

"What are you telling me?" I demanded, sitting up but still afraid to open my eyes.

"Shut up!" the voice shouted, suddenly sounding hauntingly familiar. "You're going to wake up Justy!"

CHAPTER 22

My head dropped down, and my blood felt like it was flowing colder than the rain, even colder than the waters of Purgatory Creek. *I must be dead*, I thought. *Just like Chris, just like Justine.* Maybe Tom was dead, too. Maybe I had died back there on that tree, and the first thing I ever did in the afterlife was to spring a leak.

Either that or I was hearing a ghost.

That voice! That whisper! I knew that voice, but I had never heard that voice in a whisper. And it made me wonder if I was talking to God. Or was I dealing with the devil?

Feeling neither alive nor dead, I finally rose from that dirt mound like a zombie crawling out of a grave. I was soaked and cold, but also a little mad. My aggravation became adrenaline, and I finally opened my eyes to focus on the face of the whisperer.

"You!" I said. "I thought you were dead!"

"I was never dead," Chris said, as I stared at him in disbelief.

"Where is Justine?" I asked.

"She's asleep."

"But she looked dead," I said defiantly. "Tom said she was dead."

"She was never dead," Chris said. "I told you, she was relaxing."

"But what about that snake?" I said. "I thought the snake bit her."

"I never said no snake bit her," Chris said. "Tommy said a

snake bit her."

"Then what happened to her?"

Chris paused then said, "I can't tell you."

"You what? Tell me," I begged.

"I took something," Chris said. "And then Justy got it."

"What?" I asked. "Did you give her a disease?"

Chris shook his head. Then he pulled a small, empty bottle out of his pocket. That bottle had a black label on it.

"What is that?" I said. "Where did you get that?"

"Justy's granny," Chris said. "I swiped it. But you can't tell no-body."

"You stole it?"

"I swiped it," Chris said. "She wasn't looking."

"What did you do with it?" I said.

"Justy drank it when she was relaxing," he said. "She drank it to take her medicine."

"Medicine?" I said.

"The Benna-grill," Chris replied.

"Benadryl?" I said.

"She took a bunch of Benna-grills for her allergies," Chris said. "I dunno how many."

"So that killed her?" I said.

"No!" Chris shouted, sounding determined to right a wrong. "She's not dead. Why does everybody say she's dead? She's relaxing. That's what I told you."

"But Tom said she was dead," I said, shivering.

"Tommy ran away," Chris said with a determined tone. "I went back. I walked to those trees, and I got Justy. Then I kept walking outta those trees, and then there was this field. And this field just keeps going and going, all the way to here."

CHAPTER 23

C hris and I stopped talking. Then we simply walked, my shoes sinking into the mud of that field. Still, I almost laughed, reflecting on how I had thought Chris's whispering was either Satan or a saint. Looking at him again, I realized he was really like all of us: a mixture of both.

Why, you might even say Chris had saved the day. He went back to guard his girl, just like a male fiddler crab. And although he never mentioned it, I suppose he had also extinguished that fire, just like Smokey Bear.

With a grin, I gained a hint of respect for Chris. I had figured he was so dumb that he would have been trapped forever in the swamp. But for the first time that day, I could see that he was right about something.

Under the moonlight, this farm's field looked like endless rows of nothing. It seemed blank. Chris stopped and knelt, and that's when I finally saw Justine, lying atop the mud. I stopped and studied the curvature of her pretty face. And I could not stop thinking about how I had kissed her, Tom kissed her, and Chris kissed her, and how I had dismissed her as dead.

Justine looked messy. But I saw her head move and her left hand twitch. She wasn't awake, but she was certainly not dead.

"I'm sorry," I said solemnly, speaking mostly to myself.

Yes, I was sorry. I felt overwhelmed with all sorts of sorry sadness as my shoes sank deeper in the mud. I was sorry I had dismissed Chris and Justine as being less than worthy of my friendship.

Again, I began to walk, going away from Chris and Justine. But that became harder and harder; it was a tiring challenge to move atop that blank field. It was like being stuck in cement, a mind-numbing heaviness, feeling the weight of the world in the mud of my shoes.

Each wet, stinking step sank me deeper. Already, seeing that we were no longer in the swamp, I could hear those questions calling me again: "What have you been up to?" and "What have you accomplished?" and "How much money do you make?"

I didn't want to answer any questions.

Each wet, stinking step had me reaching for reality, but a part of me wanted to just turn around and go the other way, just like I did at the duck blind. I was finally out of the swamp, but that's also when I heard a hard truth in the memory of that dreary whisper, the most shocking of words, spoken when I was hunched down on that dirt mound, curled up like an unborn baby.

"This is not heaven."

Those words haunted me as I stared across the field. Still, I kept walking. I kept moving until, ultimately, I crossed a two-lane road.

There I finally found Tom, sitting under some pine trees. He looked as soaked as me, and obviously drained.

"Mushrooms," Tom said to me, then pulled one out of the dirty ground and tossed it towards me. "They're just like us, Apple Jelly. We're all in the dark. And just like mushrooms, we rot."

I took a deep breath as I listened, actually losing myself in Tom's words. At that point, Tom did not seem quite so ridiculous anymore. His words made sense. In fact, at that instant, all of Tom's words from that whole afternoon flooded back to me, a mind full of memories that begged to breathe in my brain.

"I know," I said solemnly, speaking mostly to myself.

Mulling over my surroundings, I let out a terribly long sigh. At last, I found my eyes wide open. I felt completely awake. I could finally see the whole world outside of the swamp.

I looked at that road.

And I saw the concrete.

"THIS SUCKS. THIS REALLY SUCKS. YOU KNOW IT SUCKS. AND I'M NOT PUTTING UP WITH IT ANYMORE. I'M SERIOUS."

ABOUT THE AUTHOR

Joe Tennis is a graduate of both Tidewater Community College and Radford University. A native of Virginia Beach, Virginia, the author has contributed articles and photos to *Blue Ridge Country*, *Bristol Herald Courier*, *The Virginian-Pilot*, *The Roanoke Times*, *Kingsport Times-News*, and *Coastal Virginia Magazine*. He has also written for *Virginia Living* and *Carolina Mountain Life*.

The author's other books include *Southwest Virginia Crossroads*, *Along Virginia's Route 58: True Tales from Beach to Bluegrass*, *Virginia Rail Trails: Crossing the Commonwealth*, *Haunts of Virginia's Blue Ridge Highlands*, *The Marble and Other Ghost Tales of Tennessee and Virginia*, and *Finding Franklin: Mystery of the Lost State Capitol*.

CPSIA information can be obtained
at www.ICGtesting.com
Printed in the USA
LVHW05s0907260918
591366LV00001B/1/P